ONE MAN'S DREAM

by Steve Blum

DORRANCE
PUBLISHING CO
EST. 1920
PITTSBURGH, PENNSYLVANIA 15238

The contents of this work, including, but not limited to, the accuracy of events, people, and places depicted; opinions expressed; permission to use previously published materials included; and any advice given or actions advocated are solely the responsibility of the author, who assumes all liability for said work and indemnifies the publisher against any claims stemming from publication of the work.

Dorrance Publishing Co
585 Alpha Drive
Suite 103
Pittsburgh, PA 15238
Visit our website at *www.dorrancebookstore.com*

ISBN: 978-1-4809-5994-1
eISBN: 978-1-4809-6017-6

This book is dedicated to my wife whose patience was very helpful toward the writing of this book.

Special thanks to John and Judy for their help.

Introduction

The mountains had pulled at Steve's very soul for the bigger part of his life. He didn't understand why but it had gotten worse every year since he was in his mid-twenties.

Then, John Long came into his life. An old man he met who was ninety-three years old with lots of stories and adventures about his life in a hidden valley somewhere in the Rocky Mountains.

Steve spent a lot of time with John and never tired of his stories. He could actually imagine himself living the stories other than John when they were told.

They became very close over one summer and fall, and before winter was over, John made him an offer. He wanted to live close to his family but had to be on his own. He had been on his own too long to be able to live with his children. He was also too old to survive by himself in the Rocky Mountains anymore, so he made Steve a proposition.

For the exchange of only Steve's place to live out his days, he would sign over all rights to his hidden valley. There wasn't anyone in his family interested in it anyway.

Steve never hesitated, feeling he had nothing to lose. He made sure John had enough money to live on, and by spring, he was on his way, knowing he could always come back if things didn't work out.

Finding the valley turned out to be just a small challenge compared to keeping it safe from both predators and humans.

He had to learn how to survive, and if not for the young dog he had taken with him, he wouldn't have.

Then, of all things, another love came into his life. The way she and her children survived upon arrival was a miracle in itself. What they had to do to keep their family and valley was beyond anything the law could or would have tolerated.

Chapter 1

It was early April 2001. Steve had left Ohio on April first and driven for five days. He hadn't tried to kill himself, even though the excitement was more than he could stand. He had learned patience over the years, though, and was just trying to enjoy the trip and scenery.

Steve was fifty years old and everyone said that he was crazy for doing what he was, which was leaving Ohio and heading for the Rocky Mountains to live in a hidden valley, supposedly no one knew the whereabouts. He was believing this more all the time because he had been two days longer on back roads looking for landmarks and such as the old man had instructed him on very clearly. Every time he was ready to give up or at least was getting badly discouraged, he would see something that was clear as a bell as to what the old man was talking about.

This particular old man was ninety-three years old. He had lived up in the mountains for most of his life. His name was John Long, and he had come back to Ohio for family and health reasons. He said it was too much work to survive in the mountains at his age and just thought he'd like to be with his children and grandchildren for the rest of his life.

Steve and John had spent a lot of time together over the past year and had gotten very close. John was always telling him about life in the mountains and his valley, and Steve never tired of it.

One evening they were talking, and Steve mentioned how he would love to see his valley. He said it was hard to grasp how anything could be as beautiful as John described. He told John he bet he missed the mountains something fierce, but John just said his memories were enough. He said he didn't have that much time left anyway and wanted to be with his family.

Steve told John how every fall, especially in the fall, the mountains always had a way of pulling on his thoughts. It seemed like they pulled on him stronger every year, but he was where he was and that's the way things were.

Two or three weeks went by, and one night they were talking when John said that he'd been thinking about things. He had made the offer that if he could live the rest of his life here, he'd take care of the place, and as long as it didn't cost him anything to live here, that he'd deed the place over to Steve. If things didn't work out, just come home and they'd work things out later.

Steve thought he sure wasn't out anything, and he was more than financially able, so they wrote up agreements, and now here he was in upstate Wyoming, Rocky Mountains.

Well, anyway, back roads had turned into cow paths and trees and rock walls. Overhangs were covering the road, or cow path, almost like a tunnel.

You'd never be able to see the road from an airplane or helicopter, he didn't think. The road was mostly flat rock, maybe fifteen feet wide at its widest and eight feet at its narrowest. It set between two hills that actually had trees and other vegetation growing on the sides, part of the time. The rest of the time, it had rock ledges that hung out over the road from one side or the other. It would be hard to make a road out of it from above without knowing it was there, and then you'd have to know what you were looking at.

The road finally ran out after about fifteen miles, made a hard right between two, big boulders, ran across a little stream, under a big overhang, and then into a deeper pocket, which had partially been hidden with smaller rocks on the sides. Inside was maybe thirty feet deep and just as wide. Outside looked like a rockslide and nothing else.

Well, he had arrived. He had another half day's hike, and if everything went well, he'd find his cabin. By now he knew it was very well-hidden.

He looked around, found enough brush to hide the entrance, made it look natural as he could, walked back to his SUV, unpacked his food and supplies for the night, made a small campfire, fed his dog, made a supper of beans and franks, and enjoyed a pot of coffee. Next, he loaded his rifle and pistol before rolling up in his bedroll and relaxing.

The food was extra good for some reason, and coffee had never tasted better.

John had said to never get to relaxed, but he couldn't help it for now. There was a fresh bowl of water in the cave coming from a spring out of the rocks. It caught in an upper pocket about a foot deep and ran over into a pocket at ground level. The dog could drink there. He knew the dog would wake him if anything came around, so he fed more wood on the fire, rolled up tight in his blanket, and went to sleep.

Chapter 2

About 2:00 A.M., Steve awoke. He was wide-awake and very alert. For a second, he just lay there and listened. Everything was dead quiet, which was probably what woke him. With his right hand, he reached for his pistol, found the grip, eased it out of the holster, and waited for about five minutes. At first, he heard nothing; then over at the end of the cave he heard the slight growl of the dog. A quiet growl that meant he was ready to fight.

He added a couple of dry sticks of wood to the fire, and pretty quickly flames shot up. He could barely see the dog against the far wall, half crouched, hair up, and looked like business. He eased out of the blankets, checked the loads in the .44 Magnum, and then added some more dry wood. Then he went over next to the dog. He could see nothing but trusted the dog that something was surely there. Then as quickly as everything began, the dog stood up straight and acted like everything was fine. "Well, Mouse," he said, "you scared the crap out of me. I ought to shoot you for lack of anything better to do right now. It wouldn't help anything, but it would sure make me feel better right now. I'd hate it later, I guess I'll see what was out there in the morning."

Mouse—what a name for 105-pound dog. He'd had a lab with pups about a week old when his daughter-in-law came carrying this little black pup from work. She worked for a local vet and said that an older lady had come carrying him in that morning. She said the puppy was lying beside her car door, so she picked him up and took him to the vet's office. Must've been a first-time mother that had the pup and then left it where it laid. Anyway, that's how it ended up at his place. They fed the puppy at the office that day, and it came to his house. Steve must have a soft heart because he took the pup out to the barn, lay it with the lab, helped it for a few seconds, and it went to nursing.

The lab had no problems taking the pup, but it was so little compared to the rest of the litter, they started calling it Mouse. They had to mix up a formula for the pup because the other pups kept pushing him out, but he finally started growing and wouldn't quit. Near as he could tell, he was part mastiff and German shepherd. Total guessing, but not far off. A big, powerful, nice-looking dog, and he sure wouldn't want him mad at him.

By now, it was going on 3:00 A.M., so he built up the fire, rolled back up in the blankets, and tried to go back to sleep. For the most part, though, there wasn't a lot of sleeping. One eye stayed open, and Mouse pacing back and forth didn't help.

Chapter 3

Next morning Steve woke up with a chill that went clear to his bones. It was colder than a well diggers butt, so to speak. He threw some wood on the coals and soon had a fire going. The fire was in a small rock overhang, so as soon as the rock started heating up the rest of the little area, he was sleeping comfortably.

He put the coffee pot on a couple of flat rocks after putting more coals between them. He pulled his blanket over his shoulders and fed some small sticks under the pot. It wasn't long before it was too hot for the blankets, so he rolled them up and started some eggs and bacon frying. He then made several pieces of toast over the fire.

When he was finished, he had four eggs and half a pound of thick-sliced, hickory-smoked bacon on the plate and toast, butter, and a pot of coffee. Later he sat back and marveled about how good breakfast was. He didn't believe he could remember ever tasting anything any better.

After about half an hour, he heated up some water, washed up the dishes, packed up his backpack, and walked out the back opening of the cave. There was a small, solar electric fence hooked to a gate about ten feet wide, which kept about everything out except mice, rats, etc. But he had put rat and mouse poison around to keep everything like that out of the SUV. He'd come back later to get the rest of his supplies.

Over the years, John had thought of and packed in most everything a person would need to live fairly comfortably with a little maintenance and upkeep.

Steve looked around at the tracks and couldn't really tell what was bothering the dog the night before, but whatever it was, he figured sooner or later they'd come in contact with it...or at least figure out what it was.

Then he looked and saw where a wide trail went between two rocks before it went around the mountain. Probably fifteen feet wide and about the same height was a ledge that hung out over the trail that kept a lot of the weather off it. John said it was hidden, and he wasn't lying so far.

He walked up for about a quarter mile, and the trail went between a split in the wall. Just about the time he thought the trail was ending, he could see light on the other end, and that was it. There was enough overhang on both sides that it was like a big cave. About halfway through the cave, he felt a wet nose and hot breath on the palm of his left hand, and his heart stopped just for a second. Lord, he hated it when that dog did that. He was pretty sure the dog knew it, too. As soon as he jumped about ten feet in the air and hollered a few profanities at the dog, well let's just say the dog didn't get any closer than ten feet of him for a while; not until he had cleaned his pants and got his wits back about him anyway.

At the other end of the cave, the valley opened up. It was about fifty feet below, maybe five hundred yards wide and two and a half or three miles long. A big lake sat right where the valley split; maybe three quarters of the way down the length of it. The two walls separated into two directions about two hundred yards wide, ending at another high wall.

The walls squared off and came back toward the middle of the lake, almost like the edge of a knife. Scattered trees, some small patches of woods, thicker but not so large and what looked like a cave that let the water run through an out of the valley. He couldn't tell much from this distance, but he was high enough he could see the beauty with clarity.

Now, where was the cabin? Scanning the walls of the valley, he could see a lot of overhangs, and there, back in the shade, he could make out a couple of horses that John so often had talked about.

Looking farther out to the left of the lake on higher ground was a big ledge. Tucked back, he could see the slight glare of something. What was it? Finally, he made out the front of a log cabin that actually sat back in against a rock wall.

After he studied it for a while, he could tell the roof was actually a large rock overhang with the log front wall sat back in under. No way to see it from above or most any angle other than right in front of it. He probably wouldn't have seen it if not for the glare from something shiny on top of the flat overhang.

He just stood there for a while and soaked up the beauty of everything. Finally, he picked up his rifle and started down the trail into the valley. By the way the trail went, he probably had at least an hour and a half before he would get to the cabin and see everything.

As he started down the trail, he could see there was a storm of sorts coming in, so he thought he had better hurry. He told the dog to come on, and if he scared him like that again, he'd shoot him. The dog kept his distance.

Chapter 4

It took another hour before he finally made his way to the base of the rock wall below where the cabin was located. The sky was getting dark; it couldn't be much past noon, so he really hurried. Now it seemed like the weather was closing in on him very fast.

Walking around the bottom edge of the wall, he finally saw a small opening, about three feet wide. As he stepped in, he could see where John had laid flat rocks in to form steps up and around a slight bend to the left. It was a sharp enough bend that you could only see about six feet ahead of yourself.

The dog had already run ahead, so he didn't waste much time. Flat stones were wedged and braced securely, so there was no problem climbing up. Just as he got to the top of the steps, he saw that the dog was dead still, staring with its back hair sticking straight up. He eased his backpack off and then took the safety off the rifle. He then eased out into the open and caught a glimpse of a mountain lion as it turned and ran up and around a slight trail, about half way up the side of the cabin wall and out of sight.

Hadn't he had enough excitement for one day? Mouse had already scared ten years off his life earlier. Looking over at the dog, he said, "I guess you've redeemed yourself. I won't shoot you today."

The cabin door was locked, or at least he thought it was until he saw a small knot tied at the end of a rope, sticking through a hole in the upper right-hand corner of the door. When he took hold of the knot, it came out with about eight inches of rope before it stopped. Pulling on the door with his left hand, and the rope with his right, the rope came out, and Steve could fill a heavy board pull up and out of a latch on the inside, releasing the door.

The door swung freely open, and he walked in, letting the dog in behind him. There was an oil lamp on the table and matches. He walked over, lit the lamp, and turned back to close the door when he noticed the snow was starting to fall.

He closed the door, telling the dog how lucky he was that a storm was coming; otherwise, he'd be sleeping outside with the cat.

He walked over to the stove, opened the door and the flue, through some kindling from the box into it, and lit it. It started easily, but he had to close the door fast and open the vents until the stovepipe and chimney warmed up, so it would start drawing properly. Once everything was working properly, he added kindling and wood. It wasn't long until the cabin was warming up quite nicely.

Now, to look things over. Everything a person could need was there. Cupboards, sink, some canned food, plates, utensils, etc. Everything was wrapped in plastic and taped up. Unbelievable—he'd have to figure out how to get running water in the house, and it wasn't really late, so why not now?

He checked his pistol for some odd reason and opened the back door of the cabin. He had the lamp in one hand and pistol in the other, telling himself he was being foolish, but John had said you couldn't be too careful. Always be alert, he had said. Be stupid and be dead, never forget that. That was his wording.

He stood there with the door open for a moment, letting his eyes adjust. He hollered at the dog, and then they stepped through the door together. Mouse never showed any alarm, so Steve walked to a bench where there was another lamp, struck a match, and lit it.

There were several other lamps on shelves, so he lit them, so he could see a large cave. The cabin just closed the cave in. It was about fifty-five degrees back there, according to a thermometer on the cave wall. John had sealed everything up very well over the years. No wonder he had stayed until he just couldn't stay any longer. Ninety-three was a little old to be taking care of yourself in a country like this.

He said he found the valley when he was in his late forties and figured on wintering here for one winter. Truth was, he was stranded in the mountains by bad weather, stumbled onto this valley, and just couldn't leave. He had stayed in the cave where the SUV was parked and while hunting for food walked into this valley. As the years went by, he just kept adding and working on whatever needed done, and every spring when things turned green, you would have had to shoot him and carry him out. He said he just got too old to live here, but he wanted to come back someday when he knew his days were over and be laid to rest. He said he had a gravesite picked out, so Steve promised he'd do everything possible to lay him to rest there. He would have to make sure he found it, come good weather. Shouldn't be a problem, as John had drawn a map.

Anyway, back from his thoughts and to matters at hand. Steve noticed some canned potatoes, green beans, peaches, soups, etc. back on shelves. There was even canned meat marked elk, moose, and mule deer. There was some jerky in plastic bags hanging where nothing could get at it, and then he saw it. There were three cloth bags hanging on wire from the cave ceiling. He cut one down and found a sugar-cured ham from a wild hog, he guessed. It was all moldy, but he had seen that before. Chances are the ham was just fine. Just slice it and trim off the mold, fry the ham, and it just didn't get any better than that. He took them out into the main cabin and walked back into the cave.

He had noticed two plastic lines going into the main cabin. He followed them on back into the cave, where they had been brought in through an opening from the side and then covered with dirt. There were two valves right there. He turned them on and heard the water start flowing. Obviously, the water supply was a lot higher because there seem to be a lot of pressure. All gravity. What else could a person ask for?

He felt the two lines, and the inside line was actually getting warm. He went back in the main cabin, turned the water off in the sink, and heard water running in a little side room he hadn't checked yet.

He opened the door, and like he said, all the comforts of home. A shower, toilet, washbasin for hand washing clothes, with hot and cold water. He'd check everything else out later, but there were no leaks in the lines, so as far as he was concerned, he was in heaven.

Steve fixed a supper of ham, canned potatoes, and green beans. The cabin was very warm, so he let the dog out. He fed him some scraps and hoped the dog would be able to find his own food before long. He knew this kind of food wasn't good for the dog, so he'd have to figure something out. He also knew that he needed the dog, if for no other reason than it would let him know if anything was around.

When Steve opened the door, there was a good four inches of snow on the ground already, so there wasn't much more could be done the rest of the day or night. He had gotten here just in time. Then he looked in some cupboards and found books and a Bible. He started reading the Bible that evening and was surprised at how interesting it was. He figured it might not help any, but it sure wasn't going to hurt anything either.

About three hours later, he heard the dog scratch on the door, so he let him in. By now there was at least another four inches of snow, so he closed the door, banked the fire, shut the vent off, and closed the damper back. Then he got his bedroll out and turned in.

In the morning, he'd oil his guns. He had checked them, and they were clean and dry, but he was going to make a habit of cleaning them on a regular basis. For that night, though, he wiped them off with a rag that was damp with oil from cleanings before. He'd seen fingerprints of light rust on guns before, so he was always careful not to touch the metal. Rust was not an option.

Chapter 5

The next morning, Steve awoke to the sound of high winds. Only thing was they sounded very far away. He opened the inside window shutters and let the light into the cabin. He could see out, but not very far. Something seemed strange, though. He stepped through the door and saw close to a foot and a half of snow…give or take. It had stopped snowing, and the wind was blowing snow off the upper ledges. It was swirling high in the air and around some in the valley, making his ability to see very difficult.

It took him a minute to realize that even though it was cold, there was little to no wind hitting him. You could hear it screaming over top of the valley and through the mountains, but for the most part, the valley was sheltered, which made it a lot more bearable.

After looking things over for a few minutes, he went back in and made a breakfast of ham and the last of his eggs, thinking he'd have to try to raise some chickens, if at all possible. Probably just a dumb thought.

Mouse was right under his feet like always, but he really didn't mind. Actually, the company was welcome, and he knew that the dog would always let him know if anything was around or not, so after breakfast, they went back into the cave to look things over more carefully.

There was another stone stairway laid up of flat rocks along the wall on the left going up, and at the top, there was a small ledge that ended at a thick, pine door. Lifting the plank lock and opening the door, there was a short cave like tunnel that went hard left and opened up onto the rock ledge that sloped out over the cabin, making a perfect roof.

Okay, now he knew how that was. He decided not to walk out onto the ledge for fear of slipping and sliding off. No sense in breaking any bones or even stoving oneself up. You had to be careful; a mistake could be fatal, even a minor one out here without any help.

Steve turned around, noticing that Mouse was staring with his nose straight out, not moving a muscle, with his nose high in the air, trying to wind something. His guess was the mountain lion. Obviously, it had a den not too far off in the rocks above, and the wind was swirling sent around. That was just a guess, but probably not a bad one. John had told him there had always been a few around, but seldom had he had any trouble with any of them. He didn't like it much when there was trouble, but what had to be had to be. The hides of three big toms were on the outside wall of the cabin. They looked to be like pretty big cats, and John said he hated to have to kill them. He hoped it wouldn't come to that either.

He hollered for Mouse to come on in, but the dog didn't move. He stepped back out and looked in the direction the dog was looking. He could see nothing but a few, shadowy places, maybe one hundred yards off and a little higher. A little closer look showed a bit of a ledge around toward a shadowed area, so he guessed it might be a den or small cave leading to one. He'd look from a different angle later. He patted the dog on the head and said come on. This time, reluctantly, the dog followed.

He closed the door and lowered the plank back in place. He went back in the cabin, built up the fire, and started cleaning his rifle and pistol. Hopefully, later today, if the weather broke, he'd be able to go back to the SUV and get the rest of his supplies. He knew there was another little rock shelter on around with a sleigh that could be pulled easily by a man. If not today, then maybe tomorrow. He also wanted to find the horses that had been left here. He knew they were broken, but for the most part, they ran free in the valley. There were plenty of shelters, water, and grass. The horses just had to dig for it at times. John said the little side valleys or fields had plenty of sunshine and water. Because the grass grew thick, with very little work, the horses could easily get to it.

In the spring, he would block the horses out of a couple of meadows, so they could grow thick and reopen them in winter, so they'd have plenty to eat in bad weather.

He had four horses total: two geldings, one mare, and a one, old stallion. He said there hadn't been any babies for several years, and he didn't really care one way or the other. He just enjoyed riding some of the trails once in a while, and the geldings were broken as a team. They could be harnessed and hooked to an old wagon he had and used to carry firewood and whatever meat plus supplies back to the cabin.

When he finished with his guns, he checked the weather. It wasn't looking a lot better, so he decided to put off going back to the SUV until next morning; that way he had all day in case anything slowed him down. He let the dog out and laid down. He decided to relax a bit before checking where his water supply was coming from and how John had run the plumbing; just little things he thought might be good to know.

He read for about an hour before he fell asleep. He woke up about noon, got dressed, and looked outside. The weather had broke, so he put on his coat, gloves, boots, and hat, loaded his rifle, and walked out. He walked down toward the lake, just looking things over. He'd seen where the horses had been, so he thought he'd try to break a hole in the ice. The ice was thick, and after about five minutes, he gave up knowing they'd been getting water somewhere and really didn't see where they'd tried to break the ice themselves anyway.

He walked around to where the water ran out of the lake and found that it ran strong enough that it didn't freeze. The horses had easy access to this, so no more worries. They had been surviving without him this long anyway, so what was he worried about?

Next, he walked down toward where the valley branched off into several, little valleys that looked like ten to fifteen acres each; openings anywhere from twenty to thirty feet wide and the rock walls, allowing access into the valleys. These were the fields John was talking about; natural fences of rock walls with no visible way in or out, other than the openings he had just walked through. There were lots of different overhangs protruding out over streams and waterholes providing shelter. A person could see the thick grass bent but still holding snow up off the ground in places.

There were plenty of windbreaks for the horses, but still no horses. He checked a half- dozen separate, small fields before noticing a patch of ground where the sun had been shining for a while.

In the middle of the field, soaking up the sunshine, were the horses. They all looked up at the same time when he stepped through the opening and into the field. Then, without interest, they went back to grazing, obviously unafraid.

He was only about fifty yards away from them and could see they were in good shape, so without wasting any more time, he turned to go back to the cabin. He only had about an hour before the sun would start going down.

When he walked out from between the split in the rocks that opened into the little valley, he stepped right into the path of a small pack of wolves. They must have been hungry because their lips turned up in a growl, and they started circling. Why in the hell hadn't he brought his pistol? It was a lot quicker than the rifle.

The closest one jumped, and a seven-millimeter round flipped him end over end, killing him instantly. Before he could work the bolt action of the rifle, the second one was on him. He caught it with the butt of the rifle and tossed it over top of himself, slammed the bolt shut, and as it jumped up and charged, Steve ran the rifle barrel down its throat and pulled the trigger. The 175-grain bullet went clear through, leaving a trail of blood and gut scattered for twenty feet in the snow. Jerking the rifle around, working the bolt action, and falling to one knee all in one motion, he almost shot Mouse. He didn't know where he had come from, but he grabbed a third big male wolf out of midair, maybe ten feet before it got on Steve. Mouse tore the throat out of the wolfe in one easy slash, and it was over as quickly as it started.

Steve stood up looked at the dog and asked, "Where the hell have you been all afternoon?" He started walking back to the cabin, and this time, when the dog walked up beside him, he reached down, patted him on the head, and rubbed his ear affectionately.

Chapter 6

Steve woke early the next morning, put wood in the stove, and started breakfast after letting Mouse out. As soon as everything was around, he headed for the SUV for the rest of his supplies.

He had thought a lot about what had happened the day before with the wolves. It wasn't like them to fight like that. Normally they would just avoid a person. They must have been hungry on top of the fact that he had walked right into the middle of all three of them. None of them knew which way to run, so they decided to fight. He had no other explanation.

After breakfast and everything was cleaned up, he got ready to leave. This time he strapped on the pistol and put the rifle over his shoulder. He went out, looked around, and saw nothing to bother him. Everything looked exactly the same as the night before.

He saw Mouse about halfway across the valley, trying to look important, he thought to himself. It seemed to him that the dog had taken on a different personality in the last few days. He was only a little over a year old, and when Steve got here, he was like a big puppy. But now, he was acting more like he was protector of all, and this was his territory. He was spending less time in the house, but always close by. He stopped once and looked directly at him for a few seconds, then went on his way.

Steve walked through the opening in the rocks, down the steps to the ground level, and around the wall to the overhang where the sleigh was stored. He placed the rifle on a bracket that had been made for just that purpose. It was built across the front of the sleigh with some dear hide stretched over the notches to protect the rifle.

Picking up the shoulder harness he started across the valley. The sleigh pulled easily over the snow, which was a wet snow, and packed enough under the runners to hold the sleigh from sinking to the earth below. It only sank about an inch or two on the wide runners before stopping. Plus, the sleigh was empty and weighed very little. With the help of snowshoes, Steve stayed on top of the snow. He doubted it would be this easy on the way back.

About half the distance to the SUV, Steve noticed the dog was walking not far to his left, trying to stay mostly where the snow wasn't so deep. For the most part, a lot of it had been blown away by the wind the morning before. The afternoon before the sun had warmed some, melting the snow just a little before turning colder and freezing it. This made the sleigh drag easily in some places but also harder to get good footing. Steve tried to stay where the snow was a little deeper and not so hard to walk.

Upon reaching the opposite side of the valley, they were under the rock shelf, which kept most of the snow from accumulating. This made things a lot easier and the sleigh follow along smoothly.

After walking another hour, he was at the cave opening that he had to go through, before he could walk around the next trail up to the cave where the SUV was hidden. There wasn't any snow here, so he parked the sleigh, took off his snowshoes, picked up his rifle, and walked on.

When he got to the SUV, everything was the way he had left it, so he unpacked everything and took it to the entrance. He then started the SUV before carrying the supplies to the sleigh. This way the battery was fully charged, all bearings were lubed, and the exhaust was free of moisture. He would do this every couple of weeks, just to make sure everything was in good, working order, in case of an emergency. No sense having to work any harder than a person needed to.

After about an hour, he was ready. With everything packed, he went back to the SUV, shut it off, unhooked the battery, closed up the cave, and left.

Pacing the rifle back on the rack, he put the shoulder straps on and started back to the cabin. It was getting cold again, which helped. What snow was left on the trail was stiff enough that the sleigh slid easily. He took his time, not wanting to get too hot, because sweating in weather like this could be deadly.

He pulled the sleigh along until he was ready to cross the valley, where he sat down to rest for a while. Watching the dog, he noticed he was pretty interested in something over toward the cabin. Steve looked hard, thought he might have seen a shadow move a little once, but that was all. Figuring the cat might be moving around some, he told himself he had better keep an eye on the dog and pay close attention to how it was acting.

He started across the valley without putting the snowshoes back on and was glad he didn't. Turned out he didn't need them now and could move faster without them.

Once the dog stopped and looked up, dead still, so he did, too. Studying everything very closely, looking for anything out of place, Steve could see nothing. For some dumb reason, he asked the dog, "What?" He knew he couldn't answer, but he asked anyway. Then he saw something move on the ledge above the cabin. There was a brown spot on the rock ledge above the cabin that was clean of snow. The tail of the mountain lion slowly moved from side to side. The rock was probably still warm from the sun, and it was just lying there sunning itself while watching Steve and the dog walking his way.

The big cat must have sensed he had been seen because he jumped up and ran about the time Steve's eyes focused on him. It ran around the overhang, jumping over a five- or six-foot, angled wall and out of sight in just a few seconds.

After that, he could just see glimpses of the cat here and there, as it ran around the ledge and disappeared into the shadows, where it disappeared right into a shadow in the wall. This is where Steve thought he could see a shadow the day before and figured this must be its den.

About that time, he saw Mouse run across the front of the cabin. How did the dog cover all that ground so quickly, and why hadn't he seen him take off in that direction?

He had been so engrossed on watching the big cat that he hadn't noticed when it took off toward the cabin.

He told himself again he really had to be careful because that cat could be above him at any time when he walked out of the cabin. It was looking like he might have to kill the cat for his own safety. He really didn't want to, and he told himself he'd cross that bridge when he came to it.

He was glad the dog couldn't get over the ledge where the cat ran because it wouldn't be any match for the cat. Thinking about it, he knew the cat would just roll over on his back in a fight, and with his back feet, he would cut the dog apart so badly that his insides would just fall out. That settled it, he thought, he would have to kill the cat.

He got back to the cabin just before dark, and it was well after by the time everything was unloaded and put away.

He fixed some meat, then mixed cornmeal in the broth for the dog before fixing his own supper. They both ate their fill, and the dog laid down by the door while Steve cleaned everything up. Then he wiped the moisture from his guns and oiled them. Laying down, he read from the Bible until he fell asleep.

Chapter 7

The next morning, Steve woke up thinking about the cat. He really didn't want to kill the thing but didn't see where he had much choice. He let the dog out and fixed himself breakfast. He wanted to go hunting today, so he started getting things around and ready to go. He had brought dog food from the SUV, so that was put out in a pan for the dog.

Mouse had eaten his fill the night before and really wasn't hungry this morning, so he placed the pan where it wouldn't get wet. Later he would boil a large pot of meat and then mix the broth with cornmeal, which he could store and dip out portions for the dog, when needed. This would keep the dog healthy and would be very sufficient for cold-weather feeding.

The sun was starting to warm the west side of the valley when Steve strapped on his handgun, picked up his rifle, checked his loads, and stepped outside.

Standing under the overhang for a few minutes, he looked the valley over, hoping to see a mule deer or an elk. *Would be nice*, he thought, to shoot it from here and not have to carry the meat any farther than he had to.

Finally, he decided to head north. He hadn't been that way and really wanted to look things over anyway. He didn't see the dog, but knew he'd be along or at least wouldn't be very far away.

He started out then and stopped dead in his tracks before he walked out from under the overhang. He went to the left, over to the rock wall, and eased out from the overhang, holding his rifle at ready. As he eased out, he tried to see over the overhang. Seeing nothing, he put the rifle back over his shoulder and pulled out his pistol. The .44 Magnum was more than enough to kill the cat, and a lot quicker in tight quarters. Holding the pistol at ready, he pulled the hammer back, so all he had to do was point and pull the trigger, if need be.

As he eased out, he could see there was nothing there, so he holstered the pistol and told himself again that he had to kill that cat.

Walking down to the valley, he started north, staying above the lake. As he walked along the bottom of the rock wall, he came to the waterfall, which fed the lake. It ran out of the rocks, about fifty feet up. There was a ledge, and from where he was standing, he couldn't tell much more than that. He would come back on the opposite side of the lake, and maybe he could see more.

The water looked to be about six feet deep, running out of the pool where the falls hit. He wasn't sure how deep the water was where it was hitting, but he knew it was deep. The mist from the falls had ice formed on the rocks and trees for a good fifty-foot radius.

Staying clear of the ice, he walked down the stream to the edge of the tree line. Here there was a place in the rocks where the water ran under a big rock slab before entering the lake. This made a natural rock bridge, and he found both deer and elk tracks on the opposite side.

Staying deep enough back in the tree line so as not to easily be seen, he crossed several game trails splitting off the main trail in which he was following. He didn't have time to check them all out today, but he knew eventually he would. For now, he just wanted to stay on the main trail.

After walking a mile or so, he could see the rock walls where the main valley ended. He noticed where the game trail went deeper into the tree line, away from the valley, so he stayed on it.

It looked like he was coming to the end of the valley and the trail sort of disappeared right into the wall of rocks.

The closer he got, he could tell there was an opening in the rocks, and the trail went right through. Standing directly in front of the wall, he could see the opening easily, but from the sides, the trees made it a lot less noticeable.

There was plenty of room to walk through; at least ten feet, and then it opened up into another smaller valley. Not nearly as big as the main valley, only about half a mile deep, but just as wide, and a lot more trees. It had good timber on the sides and about a five-acre field of grass in the center.

Looking closely along the tree line, he could see several elk. A seven-pointer standing proudly about four hundred yards from him, and he thought how nice a trophy that would be. There were several, nice, young elk, also but it was a long way back to the cabin. Next time he'd bring a packhorse, but today a young mule deer would be a lot better, if possible.

Staying where he was, he studied the field for maybe a half hour before finally seeing what he wanted. Out of the tree line on the left-hand side came several mule deer walking toward a small waterhole fed by a stream, right in the middle of the field. The last one out was a small buck, maybe 120 pounds. Just what he was looking for.

Easing the rifle over the rock, which he was standing behind and using as a rest, he quietly eased the safety off, making little to no noise whatsoever. They were only about two hundred yards off, and their hearing on a clear, quiet day, such as today, was extremely good. If it heard the click of the safety being released, it would alert them of his presence, and they would scatter.

Putting the crosshairs on the front shoulders of the young mule deer, he gently squeezed the trigger. As the rifle pushed against his shoulder, he saw the deer fold up; a good, clean kill, he thought to himself.

Steve watched the valley clean out before he moved from behind the rock. Looking behind himself, he noticed Mouse standing there; obviously, he had never been far from his side. The dog was working out well. And to think he almost left him in Ohio.

He walked over to the deer, skinned and gutted the animal, then laid the hide out flat on the ground, hair down. This way he could take all the good meat and wrap it up in the hide, making it easy to carry.

After tying everything together, he secured it to his backpack, then strapped this onto his shoulders and headed back.

He walked back on the east side of the valley, wanting to see exactly what the falls looked like. He could see the water came from about halfway up the high wall. There was a small shelf that led all the way back to the cabin and also continued on the opposite side of the water flow. He'd have to check that out as soon as possible.

He was really curious as to how the water was coming out the side of the high wall. The days were warming up enough that the snow was melting, but as soon as the sun started going down, it cooled off fast. By the time he got back and hung the meat up in the lower shed, it was almost dark. Closing the doors to the room where he hung the meat, so nothing could get to it, he went up to the cabin. He would cut it up tomorrow after it cooled out.

Walking up the steps, behind the dog, he kept his eyes on the dog as much as the shelf above the cabin. The dog showed no signs of anything wrong, and he couldn't see anything, so he went on in. He usually had a sixth sense about things anyway and felt nothing wrong, but you couldn't be too careful.

Chapter 8

The next morning, Steve ate breakfast before daylight and was out at sunup. He sat on a wooden bench and leaned back against the cabin, wall enjoying a cup of coffee. The sun was coming up over the walls surrounding the eastern part of the valley.

Lord, he thought, *this had to be as close to heaven as a person like himself could get without dying and actually going there.* Thinking about it, he thought that if God would let him, he could just stay here through eternity.

About that time, something caught his attention in the shadows of the eastern walls of the valley. Sitting there, studying intently, he kept thinking he saw movement from time to time. Looking around, he realized Mouse was nowhere close by, so he kept studying the shadows on the other side.

It was a long way across, but as the sun gradually lightened things up, he saw what he thought was the dog. Mouse was one hell of a name for a dog that weighed at least 110 pounds now. The dog had been getting leaner and stronger every day. He looked more powerful than ever. This life was absolutely agreeing with him. Thinking about it, he thought maybe he'd start calling him Moose instead of Mouse. That would surely fit better.

Then something else caught his attention. Studying the shadows, he could see another dog. *What in the hell?* he thought. Stepping back inside, he grabbed his binoculars off the peg and watched. As he watched, he could see a wolf was following Mouse. Watching closely, he thought at first the dog better be ready for a lot of trouble, but then he realized that the wolf was way too close for the dog not to know it was there.

Suddenly, the wolf jumped at the dog and grabbed at his tail. He spun, and they faced each other for a second. Then, as if on cue, they jumped at each other and then started playing. *Well, I'll be,* he thought, *looks like Mouse has found a mate.* If it had been a male wolf, he was sure the dog would have killed it.

She wasn't as big as him, but she still looked to be a pretty big wolf. *Oh well,* he thought, *good for the dog.*

After he finished his coffee, he went back in the cabin, cleaned everything up, and got ready to finish his plans for the morning. He strapped on his pistol and went outside. It was still only about thirty-five degrees, but the sun felt good.

Building a fire in the fire pit, he placed a cast-iron pot of water over the pit. The pot was hung on a pole that was wedged tightly in a small split in the rocks. There was an arm that hinged out, allowing a person to swing the pot over the fire and remove it as needed.

As the water was heating up, he went down off the ledge and retrieved one of the front quarters of the deer. By the time he had this cut up into small pieces, the water was boiling. Putting the meat in the pot and what fat he could trim off the deer, he allowed it to boil while adding wood to the fire.

Going back into the cabin, he got a bag of cornmeal and returned to the fire. Suddenly, he felt very uncomfortable about things, like he was being watched. Looking around, he could see nothing, but couldn't get over the feeling. He looked over, and his rifle was still leaning against the rock, close at hand, where he had left it. He looked on the ledge above the cabin as best he could and saw nothing.

The hair was standing up on the back of his neck, and he didn't like it. He took the holster strap off the hammer off his pistol, just in case. Standing there, studying everything closely, he saw nothing out of the ordinary. Finally, the feeling subsided, and he started to feel better. Only then did he start adding the cornmeal to the boiling water until it started getting thick. When the consistency was what he wanted, he turned the pot away from the fire.

He then placed the mixture into buckets and spun the lids on tightly. Placing the buckets beside the cabin, he put a large rock on top to secure the lids. This would keep the dog fed for a month if it stayed cool, and it would definitely keep him healthy. If the weather got too warm, he'd have to put it back in the cave where it stayed cool year-round.

Adding water to the pot, he swung it back over the fire, heating the water and adding soap, washing everything up. After everything was clean, he grabbed up his rifle and walked through the cabin, into the cave, and up the stairs onto the shelf, above the cabin.

Out on the shelf, he walked around to the left—the right side when facing the front of the cabin. From there it was easy access to the shelf above the cabin, which led to the waterfalls.

Once on the shelf, he saw where his hot water supply was coming from; there was a hot spring John had rocked up with a pipe coming into the center. He had taken cement, laid a layer of stone on the bottom, and built the rocks up on the sides for at least three feet. He had put an overflow three or four inches from the top and made a cover to keep any small animals from getting into the water. This kept the water flowing, so it remained hot.

Walking on around the ledge, he headed for the falls. The ledge was a lot wider than he had originally thought when looking from below. It was easy walking, and you could see most of the valley through the trees below; especially because there were no leaves on at this point and time. You could see different places where the openings in the east wall that went into some of the other smaller meadows. They were places he definitely wanted to explore before bad weather hit again the following winter.

He could hear the falls for at least five minutes before he came to them; at first, very faint and gradually louder, until he came to a pool of water on the shelf, approximately fifteen feet around and maybe two feet deep, before rolling over the rocks. The water came out of a cave behind the pool, and he found another plastic pipe that came into the pool. This was evidently where his cold water came from and, looking closely, he could see where the line was laid in a split in the rocks and covered, so it wouldn't freeze either.

Going back into the cave, there was a path around the pool. There was a lot of water coming from somewhere. There must be a lake above from the mountains feeding down through the rocks and into the pool. Wherever it was from, the water was clean cold and tasted sweet; that was the best he could describe it.

About ninety yards past the pool and water flow, the ledge ended, and he had to turn back, but not before studying the valley as much as possible from that viewpoint. He wanted to know everything he possibly could know before checking things out thoroughly from below.

Heading back, he started getting that uneasy feeling again, so he kept his rifle at ready, with his thumb on the safety, in case he needed it in a hurry.

Getting back to the cabin, he was on edge; so bad that he felt almost sick to his stomach. He stepped down to the ledge and looked around the corner before stepping out. Nothing! *Damn*, he thought, *what is the matter with me?* He walked across the ledge and to the door, which led to the steps and down into the cave. Going through the cave and into the cabin, everything was fine there. He opened the door of the cabin easily and looked out.

Seeing nothing, he stepped out. Why was he so edgy? The hair was standing straight up on the back of his neck. Damn it; this was making him sick to his stomach.

Watching closely, from the cabin door, he neither seen nor heard anything. He stood perfectly still for a good five minutes before stepping away from the cabin. It was way too quiet for his liking, but he could see nothing wrong. He walked out to the ledge and looked out over the valley. Seeing nothing, he set the rifle down against the rock and stood studying everything. He removed the safety strap from over the hammer of the pistol, and this is what saved his life.

Everything happened in seconds. He heard Mouse growl and saw him come from the split in the rocks where the steps led down off the ledge to the valley. Acting on the dog's reaction alone, Steve spun around, drawing the pistol at the same instant. As he spun, he caught the shadow of something coming from above him. He pointed the gun at the object and shot from the hip, feeling the pistol jerk in his hand and hearing the report of the .44 Magnum. The cat was so close that he actually saw the hair separate as the bullet entered its chest.

The cat screamed when the bullet hit him. It was his last scream, but the momentum of the leap drove him into Steve, knocking him down and almost off the ledge. The dog had him by the throat at the same instant it hit the ground, and Steve just wanted out from under the cat. He was almost free when the cat's hind legs started kicking, from either reflex or death throes, or both, but before he could get clear the claws of one hind foot caught and tore his pants and leg from his hip down to his knee.

Kicking free, he rolled away, feeling the cool air on his leg. He jumped up, ready to shoot again, knowing the cat was dead, but still ready to shoot just in case.

Grabbing the dog, he pulled him away from the cat, its hind legs now kicking viciously at nothing in particular, but it gradually kicked itself off the ledge, falling down onto the ground below.

The dog looked up at him as if to say, 'Sorry I wasn't quicker,' and then laid down at his feet. Feeling the warm, wet sensation of something running down his leg, he knew he was cut, but how badly he wasn't sure.

Limping into the cabin, he removed his pants and grabbed a clean towel from the shelf. After wetting it, he sat down to inspect the damage. There was one deep cut that ran from hip to knee, and two, smaller scratches, one on each side, which weren't nearly as bad. Luckily, just the center claw had done any real damage.

Chapter 9

Steve sat back for just a minute to let the blood flow, hoping it would help clean the cuts. His thoughts were that the blood might run some or most of the dirt out of the cut.

Then taking his shirt off, he wrapped his leg, making a tourniquet above the cut. Actually, he just tied the shirt above the cut as tight as possible trying to slow down the blood flow. Then he started cleaning the cut, so he could see just how bad it was.

He opened the vents on the stove and put some wood on the coals. Then he placed a pan of water on the stove to heat. Taking his pants off, he placed them on the floor, along with several rags to catch the blood, and soapy water, which he knew he would be spilling. Then he got his first aid kit, clean rags, peroxide, bandaging, and extra roles of medical tape.

The bleeding had slowed considerably by the time his water was ready, so he sat down and proceeded to wash his leg thoroughly. Only then could he see just how bad it was.

After everything was clean, he could tell more. The outside cuts were not much more than deep scratches, maybe an eighth of an inch deep, and were a good inch and a half away from the main cut. The center claw went deep, probably close to a half an inch or more. This was in the muscle and would take a while to heal.

Pouring peroxide on the cuts, he allowed it to clean thoroughly before wiping it off. He repeated this three times before deciding it was clean enough.

Next, he took scissors and medical tape and made bridges, or butterflies. He wasn't sure what they were called, but the idea was to hold everything together without sticking to the cut.

Wiping the skin dry at the top of the cut, he placed the sticky end of the bridge on one side of the cut and stretched it over, pulling it to the opposite side and then sticking the opposite end of the bridge, allowing it to pull the cut together. He placed a bridge about an inch or so apart down the main cut. As long as the tape held, he knew it would heal nicely.

After finishing with the main cut, he put several bridges on the smaller cuts. It only took a few of them to hold these together.

Then he poured iodine on the cut before wrapping his leg with clean bandages. After that, he untied the tourniquet to allow the blood to flow freely.

By now, it was late, so he carefully loaded the stove and shut the vents. The cabin was more than warm enough, and he didn't want to have to get up in the middle of the night to add wood.

Placing some more rags on the bed to prop his leg up, he then laid back for the night, hoping he'd be able to get some sleep.

Chapter 10

The following morning, he awoke with a small amount of pain in his leg. Not nearly as bad as he had expected, but bad enough.

Unwrapping the leg, he saw a lot of seepage, but still he knew it could have been a lot worse. He heated more water and rebandaged it. More peroxide, dried everything off, then more iodine.

While fixing breakfast, he thought how lucky he had been that the dog had alerted him of the cat. That was as close as he ever wanted to come to being killed by anything ever again. Thinking about it, he sure was glad he hadn't shot the dog for scaring him so badly in the cave that first morning when he came into the valley.

The dog always seemed to be there when needed, and his intelligence was proving to be very superior to any dog he'd ever had or been around. Just like when he shot the mule deer, he hadn't even known the dog had slipped up behind him and laid down, not making a sound. As if he'd known how important it had been to be quiet.

After about an hour, he decided the cuts had had enough air. Placing his hand on the skin next to the cut, he felt no fever, so he rewrapped the leg and decided he'd better go into town the following day for bandages and supplies. Plus, if he could, he better find a doctor, just to be safe.

He got dressed, cleaned his guns, and limped outside. He saw where Mouse, and obviously the wolf, had laid by the opening going down into the valley. They hadn't been gone long, so they must have left about the time he started stirring around inside the cabin.

Looking at the sky, he thought to himself how it looked and felt like rain. The weather had been warming up a lot every day, but it was still cold at night. *Perfect weather for storms*, he thought to himself.

He went back in and got his knives. Starting down the opening and onto the steps, he realized just how stiff his leg was getting. He guessed he better get the cat skinned and then get ready to head for town and a doctor first thing in the morning. A tetanus shot wouldn't hurt anything anyway.

When he got to the bottom, he saw the cat laying out from the ledge, about twenty feet. It had flopped a couple of times and laid still. He could see where Mouse had been there, evidently just making sure, and the tracks of the wolf were close by, but she had not gotten any closer than maybe ten feet. Obviously, she was well-educated on such things. This worried him about Mouse; he just didn't realize he could lose a fight, or maybe he just didn't care when it came to protecting him.

He grabbed hold of the cat and realized he had a big job ahead of himself. The cat must have weighed at least one hundred pounds and was stiff as a board. This wasn't going to help the skinning process.

He went around to the shed, dragging his leg, and got the cart. After loading the cat, he was finally able to work his way back to the shed. He started skinning the hind legs and then hooked a gambler to them and onto a block and tackle. This way he could cut the hide off without having to bend over anymore than he had to. He could easily raise the carcass up as needed.

Cutting the hide down the belly, he could then cut and pull it off the animal. He was thinking to himself how much easier it would have been if it wouldn't have been so cold and stiff.

When he finished, he stretched the hide and rubbed salt into the inner skin as best he could. He would be sure and get some tanning chemicals while in town.

Then he hauled the carcass away and dumped it in a ravine, figuring the buzzards had to eat, too, and he sure couldn't bury it with his leg in the shape it was in.

By the time he was finished, his leg was killing him, and he noticed it was bleeding again. He took everything back to the cabin, cleaned up the knives, and checked his leg. A few of the butterflies had come loose, so he made some more, cleaned it again, and let the air get to it for a while before wrapping it back up. Then he started getting things ready to leave for the following morning. He wanted this to heal for another day before he walked out.

Chapter 11

The next morning, he was up early. Actually, he hadn't slept much the night before. The leg hurt some, and it seemed like every time he fell asleep, he'd move wrong, and the pain would wake him up.

When the sun came up, it was still overcast, but it hadn't started raining yet. It wasn't really cold, so he rewrapped the leg, grabbed his guns, and walked out. Mouse greeted him at the door, and he caught a glimpse of the wolf as she ran through the opening off of the ledge. He never looked for her to make up to him, but as long as she never turned on him, they would get along just fine.

Steve got out some of the cornmeal mix and put it in a pan for the dog. He patted him on the head, and said, "You might want this before I get back."

Then he started walking toward the SUV. He had full intentions of looking things over to see just what had to be done to make the opening a little bigger, so he could get it through and closer to the cabin. If he could, he would bring back what was needed to make the opening bigger, or maybe he'd just get a four-wheeler and trailer while he was in town, if he could find one. It sure would make life easier. Besides, it would make it a lot better when he was looking his valley over or bringing in firewood or meat.

It took him almost five hours to get to the SUV. He wasn't walking very fast and was afraid of his bridges pulling loose. His leg was plenty stiff and hurt some, so he just took his time. He never stopped walking, and Mouse was right beside him the whole way. It was like he knew he had a problem, and he wasn't leaving his side.

He got to the SUV, hooked the batteries up, and turned the engine over. It fired right up, so he just let it run for a couple of minutes while he opened up the cave on the other end. He drove the SUV out, closed the cave back up, leaving the dog there and telling him to watch over things while he was gone, as if he understood.

After covering the rifle up on the backseat, he put the pistol in the glove box and was finally on his way to town.

It was late afternoon before he arrived in town. Upon coming to a motel, he pulled in and purchased a room. The lady at the desk told him there was a doctor's office in the little mall, right across the highway, and he would be in first thing in the morning. Steve grabbed dinner before turning in for the evening.

The next morning, he was up and waiting for the doctor when he opened his doors. He was just a little country doctor, and Steve was the first one there, so in about fifteen minutes, he was being looked at. Telling the doctor what had happened, he was told how lucky he was. After an examination, the doctor said he had done all he could do, under the circumstances. Everything looked good, so he was given a tetanus shot and some strong antibiotics.

After the doctor finished, he left out, heading east on the main highway. He remembered passing an equine and saddle shop on the way in, so he stopped and bought more salves, iodine, antibiotic soap, and sprays for horses, knowing anything that could be used on a horse, could be used on humans, although it was a lot cheaper.

Next stop was a motorcycle dealer, which was right on that same highway. Two hours after he pulled in, he drove out with a slightly used four-wheeler and trailer hooked behind his vehicle. They were both used, but in like-new condition.

After that he stopped at a couple of trading posts and got as much supplies as he could possibly haul and headed back for his valley.

By the time he was back to the cave and got the vehicle parked, it was coming dark. He closed up the cave, unhooked the batteries, and unloaded the four-wheeler. Then he unhooked the trailer from the SUV and re-hooked it to the four-wheeler. After loading everything onto the trailer, he strapped a canvas over everything and headed for the cabin.

By midnight, he had everything put away, plus the four-wheeler and trailer parked in the lower shed. By 2:00 A.M., he had eaten, cleaned up, and was in bed. The dog had met him at the cave and followed him back to the cabin. His food had been eaten, so he must have been back to the cabin, and then back to the cave periodically, waiting for his return.

He put more food out and wondered where the wolf might be. He hadn't seen her, but knew she wasn't far. His leg felt better and figured he'd probably get a good night's rest tonight.

The last thing he remembered was lying down and feeling his muscles relaxing. That was it until he woke next morning.

Chapter 12

He awoke to a howling wind and the sound of a driving rain outside the cabin. He got up and looked out at a rain that was so hard he couldn't even see to the edge where the shelf dropped off to his valley.

The rain had held off until he got back, and he was thankful for that. He stepped out and was glad for the overhang above the cabin, also. At least he had an additional twenty feet in which he could walk around outside of the cabin.

Mouse came up, wanting his pat on the head, and Steve noticed the wolf in the corner, laying as far away as possible and still out of the weather. She obviously didn't like or dislike him, but she was never going to get any closer than she was right then, he didn't think. She didn't growl, just stared, non-trusting and keeping her distance as far away as possible without going out into the storm.

Steve knew that if he walked toward her, especially while looking at her, she would run right out into the storm without hesitation. So, he just made over Mouse a little, walked around under the shelf, and ignored her completely.

He could see she was a very young wolf, and as far as wolves go, she looked nice and healthy. He figured he was safe as long as Mouse was there, but he wasn't completely convinced of that until he noticed that the dog always kept himself between him and her. That was a good sign, he thought.

After about a half hour, he put some more food out for the dogs before going in, never looking directly at the wolf.

For the rest of the day, it rained like that. He could hear the thunder all around, and that evening, he took a chair out and sat under the ledge watching the lightning dance all around the mountains. If a person liked storms, and in a weird sort of way he always had, it was a beautiful sight.

Sitting there, he thought to himself how anything so beautiful could be so dangerous and deadly. He wouldn't want to be out in this, and obviously the dogs didn't either, for they had been holed up there together all day.

For the next three weeks, the weather stayed bad. It wasn't that cold, but the air was so damp that a person had a wet, cold feeling all the time. He kept a fire going and really appreciated the hot water in the cabin. The showers really felt good at night.

About all he could do was keep his guns oiled and ready. The dogs came and went, sometimes being gone all day but always coming in about dark.

For the most part, Steve and the wolf ignored each other, but he noticed she paid very little attention to him, and if for some reason he happened to walk closer to her than normal, she paid him no mind. He knew this, but he sure as hell wasn't going to try to pet her. Some things were best left alone; leave sleeping dogs lay, so to speak.

He guessed he might be wrong about how close he'd be able to get to her, but it was definitely going to be on her terms. She was very young, probably her first year, so she wasn't very set in her ways and hadn't learned not to trust humans. He had no idea as to what had happened to the rest of her pack. Maybe she had just got separated somehow, but what he was sure of was she wasn't leaving the valley. Not as long as Mouse was alive anyway. This was her home now, and he didn't think she was going anywhere.

Chapter 13

Finally, the weather broke. It had been a week trying to. One morning he had gotten up to four inches of snow on the ground. By noon, it was melted off, and that evening, it was raining again.

This morning he had woke up to sunshine and clear skies. He saw elk and heard turkeys off somewhere in the valley.

His leg healed very nicely and wasn't badly scarred. The butterflies had held the cuts together perfectly, so it had healed without stitch marks. The scar was only about a sixteenth of an inch wide. He had made sure to exercise the leg and massage the muscle, so the stiffness was very little. It wasn't going to give him any trouble.

He was going up the valley today to look things over that he hadn't had time to look at yet. Grabbing up his rifle, he crossed the valley to the east side, then headed north. The walk felt good, and besides, it was muddy, and he didn't want to leave four-wheeler tracks everywhere.

He walked along the wall and passed the lake and openings that split off to where the horses were first. Going on he came to another opening. This one wasn't nearly as wide. Walking back into this, he found that it kept getting smaller with a rock ceiling that kept getting lower. After going about twenty yards, the opening was just big enough for a man to walk through, and the light was next to none.

He was about to turn around for lack of light when he saw a lantern on a rock shelf. Taking down the lantern and lighting it, he walked on into a small room. There he found the fire pit and stack of wood with some canned food and a small pool of water fed by a spring keeping the water fresh.

That's all there was there, but he figured it might come in very handy in case of some kind of emergency at one time or another.

Replacing the lantern, he stepped back out of the cave and into the light. He stood there, allowing his eyes to readjust to the sunlight. It was warming up some, and he liked the feel of it. It had been wet long enough.

Heading on up the valley, he found a small, game trail that looked like it led up along the rocks and maybe out of the valley. He followed it for maybe fifteen minutes, steadily going up along the outside of the ledge. It cut in between a small split and worked its way under some big tree branches, which were hiding it from the top side.

He followed the trail through some shrubs and out into an opening, finding himself on a flat at the top of the wall surrounding the valley. Looking back, a person could see the whole valley depending on which side of the brush and pine trees you were standing. Ahead was a large area of grass and what looked like thousands of acres of timber.

There had to be at least a two-hundred-acre field of grass and swamp land and a ten-acre lake right square in the middle.

He could see a fair-sized stream coming out of the timber and winding out to a wide swath before running into the lake; the same on the lower end of the lake. It just kind of turned into cattails and swampy ground right down to the tree line.

The lake itself was clean of any growth, as far as he could see. Watching the lake, you could see fish whirl in the water feeding on whatever was close to the top.

Standing there, taking in the beauty of it all, he noticed a shadow on the lake. Looking up, he saw an eagle swooping down so fast and low down toward the water that it was hard to tell what was happening at first.

All in one motion, the bird rolled his wings back and dropped his feet into the water, bringing them back out with a powerful flap of his wings. In his claws he had a pretty fair-size fish, which he took straight to a limb high in a tree and started lunch.

That had been a sight to see. Something he had seen on T.V. before, but somehow it was amazingly different to watch a real-life struggle for survival happen. He had to chuckle to himself; it was just a bad ending for the fish.

Standing there watching the eagle, he noticed it flew over something dark in the cattails he hadn't noticed before. A big bull moose raised his head up out of the water and just stood there, looking in his direction. It was in belly-deep water, and in the thick grass area, just eating, not bothering anyone. How had he not noticed?

Watching the moose for just a few minutes, he looked back at the tree line, noticing several mule deer coming down toward the lake for water. After several minutes, he turned and started back down the trail, telling himself he'd be back as soon as possible. If for no other reason than to watch the activities for a day, this was definitely paradise.

Chapter 14

Steve turned to walk back down the trail, and there was Mouse. He almost tripped over the dog, he was that close. How that dog could walk up to him without him knowing, he'd never know.

He walked through the brush and started down the trail. The dog had gone ahead of him, and he caught a glimpse of the wolf about twenty feet or so ahead of the dog, going back down the trail. *Hell,* he thought, *they had both been there with me.* He had been so intrigued with everything up there that he just hadn't noticed them sneaking up behind him. He had to watch more closely.

After reaching the bottom, he headed north on up the valley, seeing more game trails and overhangs where a person could get out of the weather, if need be.

Skirting around the high wall to the end of the valley, he noticed a sandy area where turkeys had been dusting themselves. He'd have to make some traps for them, it would be a good change of diet.

After crossing to the other side, he came to the opening that allowed access to the field where he had killed the mule deer. There in the dirt were bear tracks—big ones.

Looking carefully around, he saw nothing close by. Upon further examination, he saw the tracks had come into the valley, so he stopped and milled around for a few minutes before heading back in the direction it had come. Walking over to where he had killed the mule deer, he could see where the bear had eaten the remains.

Mouse and his mate came through the opening, acting very nervous. Even Mouse was being very cautious. They could still smell where the bear had been that morning. Mouse acted more curious than anything, but the wolf was on guard immediately. The hair on her back was standing up, and her lips curled back in a slight growl while slowly looking all around.

Walking back out and looking the tracks over more closely, he realized just what they were. He assumed a black bear, but now he knew it was much worse. The front claws marking the ground every step were a good three inches from her toes. He should've noticed right off. This was a grizzly bear, and a big one.

The only sign of tracks in the entrance between the two valleys were scratch marks from the toenails on the rocks surface. He studied every inch closely and could not make a lot of sense of it. But he's sixth sense was telling him something was wrong.

Walking out onto the dirt surface, he made a half circle, trying to intercept any clues as to what was bothering both himself and the dogs, but was seeing nothing as of yet.

Then, as he crossed a bare spot just down from where he had killed the mule deer, he saw more fresh tracks.

He just stared for a few seconds. Then studying his surroundings very closely, he looked at the dog and wolf. They were staring hard down into the little valley, as if trying to see or wind something at the same time.

Studying in the same direction the dog was staring, he could see nothing. He knew it was there, perhaps watching them, as well as them looking for him.

A damn grizzly bear, he thought, *just what I want to share my valley with*. Actually, he wasn't going to share with any grizzly bear. He decided right then and there that he would kill it as soon as possible.

So far it hadn't caused any trouble, and he wasn't going to give it a chance. Any mistakes would be fatal, and he wasn't going to make one. He wanted to enjoy the rest of his life right here in this valley in total peace, if at all possible, and that was the way of it.

It was getting late, and he only had about an hour of daylight left. There were at least two hours back to the cabin at a fast walk, providing he went straight down the middle of the valley and headed straight for the cabin. Also, he would use every bit of daylight that was left, and still it would be well after dark before getting back.

About then he heard the wolf growl and saw Mouse stiffen up, ready to fight. He readied his rifle, but nothing came. Watching the dogs with one eye, he noticed them throw their heads up and smell the air, trying to wind the bear, he assumed.

Noticing the air had shifted and the breeze was now coming from the direction of the opposite and of the smaller valley, he knew that they were absolutely winding the bear and, yes, it was time to head in now. It was too dark to do anything else other than study on how to take care of the bear tomorrow.

They walked out through the opening, and both wolf and dog seemed very glad to follow. They headed straight down the center of the valley and made pretty good time until the shadows caught up to them.

He slowed his pace when it got too dark to see, but the trail they were on was open and went straight back to the cabin, crossing the rock bridge on the upper side of the lake. He knew exactly where they were, but he just couldn't see good enough to make good time. Mouse was at his side, and the wolf followed a little ways back. She was getting friendlier all the time, and he was actually glad she was there. He watched her actions closer than the dog, knowing her being wild-like, she was would probably warn him quicker of any danger than the dog.

Chapter 15

The next morning, Steve was up and out at daybreak. He loaded the trailer with a solar fence charger, electric fencing, stakes, insulators, sledgehammer, pliers, and everything else he could think of that he might need.

Hopefully the bear was still back there and not in the main valley. After gassing up, he put the rifle on the rack of the four-wheeler and headed to the back of the valley. He knew the dogs would be along, so he didn't bother calling them.

When almost there, he looked around and, sure enough, both dog and wolf were following along behind him. This was a real comfort, for as long as they were around, he knew they would let him know if anything else was around.

He stopped the four-wheeler a little ways back from the opening, just for safety's sake. Watching the dogs, he was sure it was safe before pulling closer to the opening.

After stopping at the opening, he first took his rifle from the gun rack and walked carefully through. The dog and wolf ran along playing, unconcerned. This eased his mind considerably, so he proceeded in setting up the electric fence, across the opening.

Then he set the solar charger up above where it could get full benefit of the sun from morning until dark every day. Running wire down from charger to the fence, he proceeded to hook them together.

The next problem was hooking up the ground. Off to the side, he drove couple of ground stakes in the ground about ten feet apart and hooked them together. Then he ran a wire from their back up to the charger. After turning the charger on, he was happy to see the lights come on and hear the click of the charger working. This made him feel better.

Then he turned the charger back off, wanting it to charge all day, just to make sure the battery had enough life to last all night. He hoped the bear would touch it, and it would shock him enough to turn him. At least that was his game plan for now.

Next, he looked the inside wall over for some kind of a ledge to sit on up and away, so that he'd be out of reach of the bear.

He found just what he was looking for, but how was he going to get to it? Studying the wall closely, he could see nothing that would help him get to the top. Walking back through the opening and from the other side, he found a small game trail going to the top, about fifty yards away from the opening. A person could make his way up there without a lot of difficulty.

Grabbing some rope out of the trailer, he went up. At the top, the trail went south into the trees. *Another day*, he thought, *I'll check that out.* Turning away from the trail, he half-walked and half-climbed to the ledge he had been looking at.

When he got to where he could see the fence, there was a little, flat rock; not much, but he could stand comfortably, so he wouldn't need the ledge after all.

Thinking about it for a second, he tied the rope to a rock, just in case he needed to get down quickly. After looking around, he could see where he could get cornered easily and might need a way out of trouble if the bear happened to come down the game trail from the timberline.

Watching the valley below, he saw nothing for quite a spell. It was pretty warm that afternoon, and he figured everything was laid up in the shade or had moved out because of the bear…probably a little of both.

It was starting to cool off, the sun was starting down in the west, and the shadows were growing longer.

He was about to leave when he saw movement along the wall, just north of his location. Studying closely, he could finally make out what was coming toward him. It was a small group of wild pigs.

They were just moving slowly along, rooting up whatever they could as they went. Resting his rifle over a rock, he waited.

When they got within twenty yards or so of the fence, he picked out one, weighing maybe 150 pounds. *Perfect*, he thought, placing the crosshairs on the forehead and squeezing the trigger.

When the rifle cracked, everything ran except one. *Perfect shot*, he told himself; never even lost the squeal.

Working his way back down to the trail, he found Mouse and the wolf laying where he had split off of the trail. *No danger of anything sneaking up behind me today*, he thought.

Hurrying down the trail and into the opening, not wanting to run out of daylight, he dragged the pig to within five feet of the fence and field dressed it. Then he spread all the unwanted parts around the area no closer than five to ten feet of the fence.

After quartering the carcass, he wrapped it in rags and placed the meat on the trailer. Then he spread the hide out maybe another twenty feet or so from the fence.

The idea was for the bear to gradually work its way up to the fence and maybe touch it by accident, or with his nose out of curiosity, rather than walking directly into it. Then it would most likely stay away from the fence, rather than just plowing through it.

He still had total intentions of killing the bear, but at least for now, he hoped it wouldn't enter the main part of the valley.

The last thing he did before leaving was turn on the fence. It's started clicking strongly, so he knew it was working, but he just had to know for sure. Walking over to the fence, he stood there for a second before reaching down and gently touching the fence—nothing. *Dammit, what was wrong?* So, he took hold of it and held on for a second…still nothing.

Looking closely at the fence, he studied it, trying to see what he had forgotten. He couldn't see anything. Getting down on one knee, he thought about it for a second. He had done everything right. Reaching down, he grabbed the fence again; this time without any fear of being hit. Only difference being he had one knee on the ground. Evidently the souls of his boots weren't allowing him to be grounded because this time, it knocked him over it hit him so hard.

"Son of a bitch," he cussed, picking himself up off of the ground, and at the same time, crossing his chest and apologizing to God for the language. His right arm ached clear to the bone it hit him so hard, and his knee hurt where the current went to ground.

"Well," he said to himself as he walked to the four-wheeler, shaking his arm and wiping himself off, "it's working."

Chapter 16

When he got back, it was almost dark, so he hung the four quarters and the side meat up in the smokehouse. It was cool, so he knew they would be okay until morning.

After feeding both the dog and wolf, he went in, fixed himself a can of soup, took a shower, and went to bed.

The next morning, he took the meat down and covered it with sugar cure. This would be very good eating next winter.

Then he grabbed his rifle, checked his loads, and headed for the north end of the valley, just to check and see if the bear had been there.

It hadn't, so he went over to the east side of the main valley to explore two other smaller fields he had found. He'd go back a little later and watch for the bear. Maybe he'd get lucky and the bear problem would be over today.

He really didn't figure the bear would be out before evening anyway. It hadn't been there last night, and he really didn't figure it would be there much before late afternoon or early evening. In the evening, if the air currents were right, it would smell the remains of the pig and would show up—or at least that's what he hoped.

Skirting the east wall, he passed the cave and slipped into the canyon where he'd killed the wolves. Some of their bones were still there, but scattered where coyotes, and he supposed raccoons, opossums, and birds had most likely done the rest.

Passing the opening where he had seen the horses, he told himself he'd look it over on the way back out, if he had the time.

Staying against the south wall, he walked around the little field like area. It went back about a mile and was maybe a half-mile wide. Along the valley wall, there were mostly large boulders with game trails leading through and between.

From the rock wall, maybe fifty feet or so, the trees started; large pine trees growing, reaching to the top of the rock walls. The limbs didn't start until at least ten feet or so from the ground, making it easy to see out from under them and into the field.

There the grass was starting to green up. You could feel and hear grouse drumming from different locations. It was almost as if your heart was beating along with the beat of the birds' wings. After the trees, there was a fifteen-foot-wide stream that was clear as glass coming from the overflow of the lake. The water was deep and ran lazily down toward the end of the little field.

As he headed for the end of the field, he heard a waterfall ahead. Thinking about it, he was sure it was coming from the lake he had found earlier when he had followed the game trail up to the top.

Coming to the falls, he saw where the water was flowing off the ledge and landing right in the middle of a large pool that was at least one hundred feet around. From there, the water was flowing toward the opposite end of the field.

Walking around the pool and behind the falls, he followed a well-traveled game trail toward the end, noticing everything ended at the same place: the game trail, the field, and the stream, all right there in one place.

The game trail went through a small opening, which led up onto a ledge above where the water disappeared into the rocks.

From the ledge where he was standing, the water looked to be at least twenty feet deep. He could see the bottom easy enough but had no way of telling for sure how deep it was. Looking back toward the falls, it looked very flat, which explained why the water was so deep and moved so slowly.

A person could see fish if he watched for them, and he supposed they were some kind of trout, but had no idea what they really were.

The water just ran over the wall and rolled gently down a sloping rock, going out of sight around the corner. He told himself that was all he really needed to know. At the other side of the ledge, the trail led back down to the field. The trail was smaller, but clear and easily traveled.

After walking to the other side, he could see light coming through the trees from the rock wall on the other side. *There must be a way through to the other field where I first found the horses*, he thought.

Before he got there, he knew he was right because there were horse tracks everywhere, and he had seen very few on the other end…or at least not nearly as thick. They were obviously going through here regularly.

As he got to the wall, he could see the opening. Actually, the wall that split the two canyons just ended maybe one hundred feet before it came to the wall at the end of the two fields.

When he started through the opening, he noticed a small set of tracks. John had said there had never been any babies, but there were the tracks; they were small, and he knew this one was not very old.

He walked on through, and when he stepped out, there they were. Only thing was, there was more than he had noticed before, and more than John had said there were to start with.

Looking closely, he could see the two geldings, the mare, baby, and a yearling. Obviously, the mare had had one the year before.

About that time, the stallion saw him. It was on the other side of the horses and came running over, snorting and throwing his head, ready for a fight. This could get bad he knew.

John had said they were broke but hadn't been messed with for several years. *Here we go*, he thought, *nothing good about this.*

Leaning his rifle against the wall, he loosened the strap from the pistol. He didn't want to but damned if he would be stomped to death.

The stallion was old, but more than a little game. He still looked healthy and was full of fight. Standing there and talking softly and holding his hands out to his sides, keeping them down low to his sides, trying to show no threat, was all he could do, other than shooting the horse.

The stallion stopped short, snorted, and pawed at the ground. It spun and kicked from a distance, threatening him and trying to get him to run.

Steve didn't run, nor did he look the horse directly in the eyes, trying not to show any threat to the horse. It snorted, charged, stopped, and squalled. Steve stood his ground and talked softly.

Gradually, the horse quieted. Little by little, it calmed down while he talked to him. The horse gradually walked over to him, bowing his neck and snorting the whole way.

All he could do was keep talking, holding his hand out and letting the horse make all the moves. After a few, intense moments, the horse touched his muzzle on Steve's fingers, then snorted and stepped back a step. Never moving, Steve just stood there and talked softly to the animal. He knew by now what the horse was going to do, so he just waited.

Finally, the horse came over and touched his muzzle to Steve's palm while making kind of like chuckling noises coming from deep within its chest, while Steve just kept talking slowly and softly.

Steve took a step closer, easing his other hand up and gently stroking the horse's neck. The horse gradually calmed and stood quietly while being made over. While scratching his neck and in between his ears, the other horses gradually walked over for their turn.

After maybe a half an hour, they had all been made over some, and even the baby allowed itself to be petted. But the yearling would have very little to do with him. He managed to pet him on the nose for just a second, and that was the extent of it.

The baby was very curious and a lot easier. It had little fear, and after a few minutes, he was able to stroke his neck and sides. He scratched his rump and watched the baby's lower lip flop, telling him he was really enjoying it.

After a little while, he picked up his rifle and headed out of the field. He wanted to get back up on the ledge and hopefully kill the bear.

Looking around he saw both wolf and dog coming up from his backside. They had never been to far away, but for some reason, they had kept their distance. He had seen them several times that day, and they had never been any closer than maybe a hundred yards away.

Chapter 17

Now that Steve was heading back up the valley, both dog and wolf came up beside him, as if they knew exactly where he was going. It was time!

He started toward the opening and noticed the wolf stop and lay down flat on her belly, with ears back and teeth showing in a low growl that could barely be heard.

He took another careful step toward the opening and felt something grab his pant leg and pull. He looked down and saw that Mouse had a hold and wasn't letting go.

About that time, the hair stood up on the back of his neck, and he knew the bear was there. He ran back along the rocks and up the small game trail, which led to the larger game trail at the top of the rocks.

When he started that way, the dog let him go, as if the dog knew he wasn't going through the opening. Sometimes his intelligence was a little scary.

As fast and quietly as he possibly could, he made the top and started easing along, trying to get to the rock ledge without making any noise.

The sun was on the west side now, so the shadows were cast on the opposite direction, and he didn't have to worry about that.

Easing into the little pocket where he could stand, he checked his loads. His rifle was fully loaded, which he knew, but checking was always a good idea while giving him peace of mind.

He eased his head over the rocks, just in time to see the bear dragging the hide back into the fence. The fence hit the bear hard, making a loud enough crack that he heard it from above. Just a loud snap, and the bear roared and jumped clear over the hide. Spinning, he stumbled and rolled, then jumped up with a vicious roar.

He was mad now and took his fury out on the hide, jumping on it and ripping it like it was no more than a piece of paper. That in itself was worth seeing, and he would have laughed out loud, if he dared.

The bear's jaws were slamming closed so hard on the hide that it reminded Steve of a steel trap slamming shut. This thing was mad and was ready to destroy anything and everything in sight.

Then the bear walked over and put his wet nose on the fence. It hit him again, and this time, he jumped back so hard he actually hit on his backside and rolled over backwards.

Standing up on his back legs, he voiced his fury. This was what Steve was waiting for. His crosshairs touched the center of the bear's chest, and he felt the kick of the rifle slam against his shoulder.

The bear flipped over backwards and landed on his belly as if someone had belly slammed him to the ground.

If the bear hadn't been so mad before he had gotten shot, Steve was sure he would have laid there and never gotten up. But along with the anger and the adrenaline, it jumped back up, and before he could get another shot into him, he charged through the fence. He must've thought, in his mind, that the fence was the whole problem, and he set out to destroy it.

They say these bears have a slow heartbeat, and he thought to himself that this must be true because it wasn't getting in any hurry to die.

Steve was perfectly content with staying right where he was and waiting it out. He knew exactly where he had placed the bullet and that it was just a matter of time before the bear would calm down and then the heart would quit.

About that time, he heard the fight on the opposite side of the wall. Hurriedly, he replaced the spent cartridge and ran back over the rocks and to the game trail as fast as possible.

When he got down the trail, dog and wolf were darting in and out at the bear, trying to keep him occupied long enough that it couldn't concentrate on just one. One would grab hold of his backside as soon as it would turn and grab at the other. They were working like a perfect team.

Trying to shoot the bear again without hitting either dog or wolf was near impossible, but finally he got his opening and shot. The bear was spinning after the wolf and spun right into his crosshairs. As the shoulders came into the scope and the crosshairs touched where the heart should be, he squeezed the trigger. The rifle roared, and the bear was knocked in the opposite direction but continued spinning.

Working the bolt action of the rifle, he chambered another round and was able to put another round on the opposite side, same location.

This time his front legs folded, and he went down but came right back up. It located where the shots were coming from and headed straight at Steve.

Working his last shell into the chamber, he quickly aimed at the bear's nose, knowing he had to lead the bear as fast as it was coming at him. Too many times, people had overshot their target in circumstances just like this. This time, though, when the rifle cracked, the bear went down. The bullet hit the backbone, right between the shoulder blades.

When he walked up to the bear, it was still alive but couldn't move anything other than its head, eyes, and jaws. That was bad enough to look at.

Pulling out his pistol, he shot the animal in the brains, ending everything. Then he reloaded his rifle, telling himself he'd really like to meet whoever it was that made the law stating that a magnum rifle could only hold three rounds. It was a stupid law, and right now, he would damn sure tell the person what he thought of it.

While reloading both rifle and pistol, he started to shake. He hadn't had time to be scared before but was now shaking like a dog crapping peach seeds. He sat down and tried to relax for a minute. It was a good half an hour before he felt comfortable enough to check his shots, just to see for sure where they were located.

The second and third shot had hit in the shoulders and looked as if they were headed straight into the heart. The fourth shot had stopped him, like he had thought, right between the shoulder blades, severing the spine.

It took a while to pull the bear over, so he could examine his first shot, but he was finally able to do so. There was the problem. He had been shooting down at a very sharp angle, which changed how gravity was pulling on the bullet and caused the flight of the bullet to be a little higher than it regularly would have been. It looked like it probably clipped the top or just missed the heart instead of finding the center of it. He would never make that mistake again.

By the time he got the bear skinned, it was dark. He'd come back in the morning with the four-wheeler and trailer to clean everything up.

Heading back, he noticed Mouse was on his right side, walking along, but what surprised him was the wolf was on his left. She wasn't crowding him like Mouse always did, but still only three or four feet away. She must have decided that he'd do because from that day on, she was always close.

Chapter 18

The next morning, Steve was up before daylight. After breakfast, he cleaned an oiled both rifle and pistol before leaving the cabin. It was almost daylight, and he wanted to be back before noon.

Taking the four-wheeler and trailer, he headed north, up the valley, arriving right at daybreak. Upon arrival, he looked around, spotting both dog and wolf close behind. This was comforting for some reason; he guessed he just didn't feel quite so alone when they were there. He knew that it was highly unlikely anything would slip up on him unnoticed when they were around.

After rolling and tying the hide as tight as possible, he proceeded to roll it up into the trailer. After that, he gathered up all the fence material and placed it beside the hide.

He studied on the carcass for a moment before deciding to take the best of the meat back with him. He would cut the meat up and cook it completely, making sure it was cooked all the way through. This way there would be no parasites, and he'd be able to cook up more food for both dog and wolf.

He had no intentions of eating any of it himself, but he knew it would be fine for the both of them.

After everything was cleaned up to his satisfaction, he headed back to the cabin and went to work. He stretched the hide first, then cut the meat into strips. Then he built a fire in the smokehouse, allowing it to burn down to just hot coals.

After that, he covered the coals with the thick layer of hardwood sawdust and hung the meat inside before closing the smokehouse up tight. He would keep the coals hot and the sawdust smoldering, making lots of smoke and allowing the heat to cook the bear meat until it was thoroughly cooked.

When he knew it was thoroughly cooked, he would pack it up and hang it in the cave behind the cabin; but for now, he had a hide to scrape.

After the hide was clean of all fat, he treated it, so the hair would set firmly. This would make a nice rug in the cabin once it was finished.

The following day was spent cutting poles for a corral for the horses. He wanted to spend some time with them, just so he could get them used to him. He hadn't decided whether he'd ever ride them or not let alone break the young ones, but it would be nice to be able to handle them if he decided he might want to. At least he'd be that far ahead of the game.

Upon completion of the corral, he built a fence that ran back to the field where the horses had been staying. This way he just had to head them down toward the corral and close the gates behind them. After feeding them a little corn, it would be no problem getting them in.

While doing this, he cut and stacked all the extra pieces into firewood. This way he could gather them up and transport them easily to the cabin later. Plus, he would take a load in with him at the end of every day.

By the time he was finished with the fence and clearing for the fence, he had at least twenty cords of wood put up for winter.

During this time, he had noticed the wolf was going to welp. There was a bit of a hole in the wall, more like a small cave area that was mostly hidden by firewood on the north and of the cabin. It surprised him when she started spending a lot of time there. He really didn't figure she would welp this close, but she did.

One evening, while sitting on the shelf, relaxing, smoking his pipe and looking over his valley just enjoying everything, he heard the tiny squeals of puppies nursing. Mouse was lying beside him and paid little attention other than lifting his head and looking that way before laying it back down.

Steve just sat back and sipped his coffee while enjoying his pipe and watching the sun go down.

He laid food and a pan of water there for her on the second day, knowing she wouldn't come out much before that. The food and water would be gone every morning, so unless Mouse was eating it at night, she was okay.

One evening, about two weeks later, while sitting in the same chair, enjoying his coffee and pipe, she came out and laid down on his left side about five feet from him. She looked at him, and he spoke softly to her, asking her if she had had all she could stand for a while. She just laid there with her head on her front legs and went to sleep.

About half an hour went by before Mouse got up and left the ledge. She got up and followed, only to return about an hour later, going back to the pups.

A couple of weeks later, they started crawling out from behind the wood pile, so Steve put some rocks around the ledge, just in case they got too close. He didn't figure they would, but it was too far to fall in case they did.

The rest of the summer was spent getting food and everything else he could think of prepared for winter. He knew he'd be snowed in for the bigger part of it, depending on how bad the weather would get. He wanted to do more exploring, but first things first.

He took a few more trips into town, buying potatoes, soups, and the like; extra clothes, shells, and everything else he could possibly think of that he might need.

He stopped in at the post office where John had had a post office box, and he paid up for another year. There was a letter from John saying his health was failing and not to forget his promise as to where to put his ashes. There was a place he had fixed up behind the cabin; he wanted the vase placed overlooking the valley. It was supposed to be delivered to him by one of his great-grandchildren, and Steve had promised to take care of everything.

He had also gotten mail from his children and grandchildren. Taking everything back to the cabin, he read and answered every letter. Then he took the return mail back and mailed it all out the following week. He told everyone if they ever wanted to visit to please let him know ahead of time and he'd make arrangements to get them here. When weather permitted, he'd check his mail at least once a month.

The rest of the time was spent fishing and hunting, smoking the fish, and curing the meat. He smoked several turkeys and sugar cured several wild pigs. He lost track of how many trout he had smoked.

He had several books to read, plus he had full intentions of reading and studying the Bible, which in his mind was very important to him. That, he thought, was up to every individual; you either believed or you didn't. Everyone in this country has the right to believe however they wanted, and in Steve's case, he did believe.

Once everything was ready, he was able to go back up on the ledge above the cabin and follow it to the south. The trail wasn't nearly as wide but easily passable on foot. He followed it around and found several small caves. One went back several feet before curving around and ending in a little pocket about six feet in diameter. It still smelled of the cat, so there was no doubt that this had been its den.

Following the trail on around, he found where he could get up out of the valley with very little effort. The top was flat for a while; maybe one hundred yards or so, then it went into more mountains. You could see snow on the tops of these, and he wandered if it had ever melted off. It was a beautiful sight.

For the most part, the flat went around his valley with patches of trees here and there, with large rocks scattered around and pine trees that grew straight and tall all the way back to the higher country. He decided then he would break the horses, wanting to be able to ride this country. He could cover a lot of bad ground on horseback while taking his time and looking the country over.

Getting back in time to enjoy the sunset in the evening was getting to be a ritual. He looked forward to the evenings, and very seldom did he not sit there with coffee, pipe, dog, wolf, and pups underfoot.

The pups were getting big now, and one was more dog then wolf. He was bigger, stronger, and looked more like his dad than the other three. There was one other thing about him. He was more flexible than the other three. His back seemed to bend a lot easier than the other three. They had stiffer backs and didn't seem to be able to twist around and grab things behind themselves nearly as quickly or easily as it could. This made it a lot harder for the other three to get the best of him when fighting amongst themselves for the dominant role. He was definitely the top dog of the four, so to speak.

Chapter 19

It was now September, and the weather was changing fast. He noticed that the dogs were staying away more all the time. Even Mouse was not to be seen for days at a time.

He was spending a lot of time with the horses now, just to have something to do. The yearling was coming along nicely; she was quiet and curious about things.

Just by standing in the center of the pen and ignoring her while working on a halter, bridal, or saddle, she had gradually worked her way over to him just to see what he was doing and gradually allowed herself to be brushed and made over.

After half a day of brushing and making over the yearling, he was gradually able to work his way up to its head and ears.

With a lot of talking and slow movements, he was able to slip the halter over its head and ears before buckling it in place.

Upon realizing that the halter was in place, it took off running around the round pen while shaking its head in protest.

After a minute or so, she gradually quieted and just stared at Steve as if to say, 'You pulled a fast one on me.'

Steve just ignored her, and after a while, she relaxed and gradually walked back over to him, looking for more attention.

While talking gently and brushing her neck, he was able to snap a twenty-five-foot lunge line on the halter. He let it hang there, with her not even realizing that it was hooked on to her.

Carefully rolling the lunge line up in such a way as it would not get tangled in his hand, he walked about five feet away from her. Standing there with his back to her, he put little to no pressure on the lunge line at all.

After a few seconds, she followed stopping beside him. He made over her again while talking to her in a calm and natural voice.

This was done several times before trying to walk away and actually leading her. Upon realizing there was pressure on the halter, she planted her feet and stopped. Standing there while facing her with a small amount of pressure on the line and gently talking to her, he patiently waited.

Gradually, she eased to the pressure and took a step forward. Taking up the slack, she stopped again, but this time not quite as long. Steve took another step, and so did she while letting the line hang loose. No pressure other than the weight of the line.

Turning, he slowly walked away, and she came along with him, not closing the gap, but not fighting or trying to get away, either.

He stopped and faced her. This time he spoke softly, asking her to come closer while he put slight pressure on the line. She hesitated for just a second before coming with the line as he rolled it up into his hand.

She came up to him and stopped where he could pet her. He made over her for a few seconds before he noticed the muscles in her body were getting tight. He knew she was getting ready to throw a fit, but for what reason, he wasn't sure. Probably just realizing she didn't really want to yield to him.

She had been in the wild, so to speak, all of her life and wasn't sure all of a sudden why she was trusting him. Suddenly she bolted away from him.

When she came to the end of the lunge line, he planted his feet and pulled her head around toward him. She swung around, facing him with all four feet planted solid with no intentions of moving.

They just stood there, facing each other for a few minutes, before either yielded. Finally, Steve let up just a little, so she would have nothing to fight. She backed up, and he went with her, not allowing any pressure on the lunge line; nothing to fight was the whole idea.

Gradually, she stopped backing up, and he was able to walk slowly up to her while talking gently to her the whole time.

Rolling the line up as he walked toward her, he gradually stepped up to her. He stood there talking to her for a few minutes before he seen her start to relax again.

Then he started over with the whole process. Slow and easy, only this time she was more cooperative, and by the time he was finished, she was leading very well.

The whole process took well over a half a day, but now he had a yearling that led along without any fear of him. He led her around while he picked up rocks and through them out of the corral with no reaction from her by the time he was finished.

He spent several hours with her after separating her from the others before taking the halter back off and putting her back in with the others.

He would repeat this several times before the weather got bad. He still wanted to build a feed room and fill it, just in case they needed a little extra feed this winter.

He gave them all a couple of ears of corn before turning them out to pasture and heading back up to the cabin for his evening coffee and pipe. He looked forward to that more and more each day and found himself in a bad mood if something happened that stopped him from enjoying his evening on the ledge, overlooking the valley.

This evening, while finishing his coffee and pipe, he noticed something staggering along on the other side of the valley. Back toward the lake, something was more crawling than walking, heading towards the cabin. Grabbing his field glasses, he tried to see just what it was.

After focusing the field glasses, he came to the realization it was one of the pups. He couldn't tell for sure which one from that distance, but he was sure it was his favorite.

Chapter 20

Grabbing his rifle and pistol, he ran to the four-wheeler. Then he hooked the trailer up, and after placing straw and an old blanket in the bed, he hurried to the pup.

He was at the pup's side within fifteen minutes of spotting him. It was mud and blood from one end to the other. He saw no broken bones, but there were deep cuts all over. He had no idea what had happened, but if he were to save this pup, he had to go to work now.

After sliding a blanket under the pup, he lifted him onto the trailer. He looked around and saw nothing of the others, so he headed back to the cabin, making the ride as comfortable as possible.

He stopped at a section of fence where the horses spent a lot of time rubbing, and he grabbed some tail hair that was wrapped around some of the fence post and poles. This would do for stitches.

When he got to the cabin, he carried him up and laid him next to the door. He went in and placed a pan of water on the stove to boil. While the water was warming, he fixed a bed inside for the pup and then put the tail hair in the boiling water to sterilize it.

After this was done, he hung the hair on a chair and added enough cold water to the hot so as not to burn the pup. Then, with disinfectant soap, he began washing the pup's wounds. The cuts were worse than he thought. They were long and deep; he could see them after he got all the filth off. That's when he realized the pup had gotten into some wild pigs somewhere.

He didn't know how the pup had survived, or even if he would. He wondered what kind of shape the rest of them were in. If they didn't show up tonight, he would look for them tomorrow. That's all he could do for now.

He worked on the pup half the night, cleaning and sewing. When finished, he poured iodine on the cuts and gave him a shot of antibiotics. He doubted the pup would make it, but at least now he had a chance.

He really didn't understand how the pup had gotten into a fight with wild pigs anyway. A person wouldn't think a young pup would just fly into a fight with a bunch of wild hogs. That would be as dangerous as anything he could think of. They could run past something and with the turn of their head, their tusks could rip an animal from one end to the other, and it looked like more than one had ran past and over top of this pup. He had no idea how it had survived.

The next morning it was still alive, but barely. Taking a soft plastic tube, he ran it down the pup's throat. Then, he filled a syringe with water several times, putting at least a pint of water directly into his stomach. An hour later, he gave him some chicken broth the same way.

He repeated this an hour later, then went out to see if he could figure out where the pup had come from and maybe what had happened to the rest of them.

He went back to where he picked the pup up and backtracked him to the game trail on the opposite side of the lake leading to the top of the east wall, just north of the lake.

A person could easy enough track him where he came down the trail. He had slid, rolled, and bled most of the way down, leaving hair and blood all the way.

On top, you could see where he had laid for a while and rested before continuing on.

Steve stood there for a couple of minutes, looking everything over closely. Then he gradually saw a slight trail in the tall grass where it was slightly bent over, laying toward him. This is the way the pup had come home he knew.

Checking the grass, he found traces of dried blood and hair before deciding for sure that he was right, then he stood up on a high spot and studied the grass.

From there, he could follow the pup's trail from the timber to where he stood. The grass was bent just enough that he could tell how he had come through.

Studying where the pup had come out of the timber, he took a different route to the location so as not to disturb the grass where the pup had come through. Arriving where the pup had left the timber, he circled around and found blood on some branches and leaves.

He could see leaves and pine needles that were turned over easy enough but needed to make sure he had the right trail.

Following this, he could move a lot faster, and within a half hour, he veered around a rock ledge and down into a small swell. There he could see up under a rock ledge and a spring running out of the rocks and down into a mud hole.

There were wild pig signs everywhere. They'd been rooting around and making a mess in general. They had a spot dug up probably fifty feet in diameter.

It was going to be hard to track anything out of here, he told himself. He walked around and studied everything from several angles.

Finally, he noticed a dog track among the pig tracks going around a rock and up in a little shelter like area.

It was dry up there, and a perfect place to get out of bad weather, but there was only one way in and out.

This is where he found everything. It looked to him like Mouse and family had been in the shelter when the pigs had come running in. The fight started there. He didn't know why it started, but this is where it happened.

The three pups were scattered and dead. Their sides ripped beyond any repair. They were actually torn to pieces by the hogs.

Mouse had gotten onto a ledge, about three feet up off the floor, but the damage was done. His side was ripped wide open, and his insides were spilled out.

The wolf was lying beside him with her head on his neck, looking at Steve. She was still alive but had not left her mate. Walking over to her, she raised her head and looked at him sadly. She didn't growl, just made a kind of whine for help.

Then he saw Mouse's eyes open. He couldn't believe he was still alive. He knew he couldn't save him, but at least he could pet him on the head one last time and say goodbye.

The dog tried to lift his head but had no strength left. Steve put his hand on his head, and it seemed to comfort him some.

While stroking the dog's head, he looked the wolf over and could see where she had fought savagely to keep the pigs off the ledge. She was cut up but hadn't gotten ripped up by any tusks. She had lost a couple of toes on her right front foot, and the hair was torn out from several spots on her front legs and chest. One ear was sliced in half, but it was still there. She was a mess but was going to be okay.

Mouse made a whimper, and Steve looked back down talking to him while trying to comfort him. He was past feeling any pain, he told himself, because his eyes were getting glassy.

Steve thought about putting him out of any misery he might be in, but he saw that there was no need.

It seemed as if his being there comforted the dog because he just kind of relaxed after he talked to him and stroked his head for a couple of minutes. He had licked his hand, which Steve had always hated, and took one last deep breath and passed.

This was really hard for Steve. He had liked the dog a hell of a lot more than he had realized, plus the fact the dog and saved his hide more than once. He was going to miss him.

Chapter 21

He carried the pups over to where Mouse lay and placed them down together, below the ledge. The wolf just laid there with her head laying on the dog's neck. He wasn't sure what he was going to do with her. He carried rocks and covered the pups, then he covered Mouse so buzzards or large rodents couldn't get to them.

Then he started stoning the opening of the shelter closed, so the pigs couldn't get back in. Before closing the shelter completely up, he spoke to the wolf. Reluctantly, she came to him.

He finished closing the shelter and headed back. The sky was clouding over, and there looked to be another storm coming in.

Steve made good time getting back to the cabin. He needed to get back to the pup anyway. He thought it was odd that the wolf stayed right at his heels all the way back to the game trail leading back down into the valley.

As badly hurt as she was, she kept up. She went along pretty well on three legs and surprised him by staying right with him.

Taking the game trail down into the valley, he noticed her having some trouble going down, but she made it without help. At the bottom, he stopped to let her rest a little and was surprised when she came over and laid down next to him. That would never happen again.

They sat there for maybe five minutes before she got up. He got up also and started for the cabin, but she just stood there.

He looked at her and asked a question: "Are you coming or not?" She turned and headed toward the north end of the valley. "Good luck," he said under his breath, and headed for the cabin.

When he got on the ledge, he stood there for a second before going in, thinking about how quickly things could change.

When he stepped in, the pup looked up at him. *A good sign*, he thought to himself. *Now if he doesn't get any infection he thought, he might make it.*

He got the pup some water, which he rolled up long enough to drink. Then he mixed some of the cornmeal with chicken broth and set that in front of the pup. He ate just a little before laying back over. Steve fixed himself supper, and after eating, he took his coffee and pipe out on the ledge and tried to enjoy what was left of the evening.

It was almost dark, and the storm was going to be there before morning. Sitting there, taking it all in and just thinking about everything, he heard the cry of the wolf. It sounded like she was about where they had killed the grizzly. He wondered to himself if he would ever see or hear anything of her again.

He told himself that if she stayed in the valley he'd leave a little extra for her whenever he killed a deer, or anything else for that matter. Maybe just knock a small deer down for this fall, just so she had something to eat while she was healing.

Chapter 22

The next morning, the pup had eaten all his food. He was still weak but improving rapidly. He wanted out, so he allowed him to go. He got up slowly and eased his way through the door. He was stiff and sore, but his strength was coming back. He gave him another pan of food under the overhang, figuring he'd be better off outside anyway.

The pup ate a little before he went back in by the woodpile where he had been born. Grabbing his rifle, he went out. It was raining, but not hard, so he thought he'd go to the north end of the valley and hopefully kill a small deer.

When he got to where he had killed the grizzly, he eased into the side valley and found the wolf tracks on the other side. She hadn't been there long before him, or the tracks would've had a little water in them.

He walked the perimeter of the side valley, just checking for game trails and to see what other ways there were or might be in and out of the valley.

Finding a well-worn trail, he followed it up and out. This led him to the north end of the main valley, and from there, he could see where he had come out when he walked from the cave in which the cat had his home. All the ways in and out were good to know.

The trail on top split and went around, skirting the top walls of both valleys. From there it looked like you could walk around the smaller valley, following the trail to the east. He'd check this out when the weather wasn't so bad.

It was raining harder, and the temperature was dropping. He didn't want to be out in this much longer. He went back down to the side valley and started a straight line back across to the opening.

Walking through a small thicket of pine trees, several deer jumped and ran out into the open, maybe two hundred fifty yards out before stopping and looking back.

Picking out a young buck, he killed it. He hurried over to it and skinned the hindquarters out. Then he took the tenderloins and strapped them in his backpack.

Taking out a short section of rope, he tied it to the deer and pulled it to the opening, going back through to the main valley, remembering a little cave not more than four feet deep and not even that big around in the wall just north of the opening on the inside of the main valley. Here he untied the rest of the deer and started to leave when he saw the wolf.

She came to the opening as he was walking away. She laid down and watched him, not coming any closer, so he rolled up his rope and headed back to the cabin. He got about fifty yards away when he looked back and saw her walking over to the deer. At least that would give her something to eat while she was healing.

He figured she would probably leave the valley eventually, but really had no idea. She had helped with the bear that day and made up to him for the most part, so he would at least help her get healthy again.

He really hoped she would never cause him any problems where he would have to destroy her. As long as she didn't, she was more than welcome here.

When he got back to the cabin, the rain was turning to snow, and it was damn miserable out. He hung the hindquarters in the smoke-house and then went up to the cabin.

The pup came out, so he stacked some wood out from the hole, just to help keep the air out. He went in and built a fire before taking a hot shower just to knock the chill off. Then he made coffee and sat back with his pipe to relax and wait out the storm.

In no time at all, the cabin was toasty warm, and he fell asleep, not waking up until almost dark. It was starting to get bad in the Rockies, and he hoped he'd have a few more good days to spend with the horses before bad weather set in. It was his first winter here, and he really had no idea what to expect.

Chapter 23

As it turned out, the weather got a little nicer about a week later. The pup was a lot better, and he was able to take the stitches out.

The pup never wanted back inside, but he seemed to have formed a stronger bond with him. Whenever he came out, the pup was beside him and never got very far from him. Even when he worked with the horses, the pup would lay beside the gate and watch him intently.

If anything came close to the cabin, the pup let him know with a growl, then as soon as he let him know that he'd seen it, he'd get quiet and moved to the side, looking ready for whatever might happen.

One day the pup gave his warning, and Steve saw a large moose at the lake. As always, the pup stepped off to the side. Steve had plenty of meat, so he just stood there and watched this magnificent animal bury his head under the water and bring out mouthful after mouthful of grass from the water's edge.

Suddenly, he noticed the pup coming around the side of the lake, sneaking up on the animal. He whistled, and the pup stopped. He whistled again, and this time, the pup came back to him.

He didn't know exactly what the pup had in mind, but it probably wouldn't have worked out well for the pup.

The pup was about six months old now and already weighed a good sixty pounds. He looked more like his dad than a wolf, but he still had a lot of his mom's features. The pup was going to be able to more than take care of himself, but he wasn't ready to tackle a moose just yet.

The pup watched the moose all day, with little else on his mind. Obviously, the pup thought he could handle the moose, or at least he wasn't sure that he couldn't.

Steve went on working with the horses and getting everything else ready for winter. He knew it wouldn't be long now before the snow would cover the ground and keep it covered.

He guessed he was ready. He had plenty of food, coffee, and tobacco. Firewood was stacked under the overhang, and he knew of no air leaks in the cabin. Water lines were covered and sealed. He was as ready as he was going to be.

He put the horses out in the canyon where the overhangs, water, and grass were plentiful. They were healthy and fat, and if he needed to, he had enough corn to supplement some. He hadn't got a corncrib built, but they had survived without it before.

Yes, he guessed it was as good as it was going to get.

Chapter 24

And come it did. There were breaks here and there, but for the most part, it was cold. The sun would hit in the side canyons, keeping a lot of the snow melted, but not all. For the most part, though, there wasn't a lot of wind.

What wind there was came out of the west blowing over the cabin and piling the snow up against the eastern wall, keeping a lot of the grass clean where the horses could get to it easily.

There was a lot of drifting in front of the cabin, swirling down from the ledges above. The nice thing was the sun warmed the rock walls, which helped keep the snow melted and away from the cabin.

There wasn't so much snow that one couldn't get around most of the time, but there wasn't much sense going out in the stuff, unless something really needed done.

Bad weather would come in, and in a couple of days, you could usually get out for a day or two and do things.

Then one night during a bad snowstorm, he heard a plane coming over. The wind was blowing hard, but between gusts, you could hear the engines clearly. Something didn't sound right.

They were laboring hard like they weren't getting enough fuel or something, and it sounded like the plane was way too low. The wings were probably covered with ice, and he guessed it was coming down.

"Why would anyone in their right mind be flying in this kind of weather anyway?" he asked himself. Stuck on stupid was all he could think of.

Jumping up out of bed, he ran to the door and stepped out. The moon was bright, and with the snow on, he could see the plane coming over the southern end of the valley, just above where his SUV was hidden in the cave.

It was barely high enough to make the wall, and if it didn't gain a little altitude, it wouldn't make the wall at the opposite end.

Watching intently, he forgot he was half-naked standing in weather that was no more than ten or fifteen degrees at best. The wind out in the open would freeze a person to death pretty fast if he wasn't dressed for it.

Holding his breath and gritting his teeth, he watched as the plane flew in front of him and headed for the wall at the northeast end of the valley. As it got to the lake, it banked easterly toward a game trail, leading up to the top where he had buried Mouse and his pups.

He couldn't believe what was happening. It didn't look like the plane was going to make it.

The wind was throwing the plane around, and he could tell the pilot was doing everything humanly possible to clear the wall.

Turned out, the plane was just high enough to clear the wall, but the landing gear was not. With a crashing sound that could be heard clearly above the wind, the landing gear was torn off the bottom of the plane, and it fell to the bottom of the rock wall, landing in the valley.

The last thing he saw was the plane going between some rocks and the wings ripping back coming free of the plane. The wings flipped up in the air, catching the moonlight and throwing a reflection back at him.

That was all he could tell about the crash from that point on. He went back in the cabin and got dressed as quickly as possible, grabbing snowshoes, a rifle, and a first aid kit. He doubted anyone would be alive, but one never knew.

He went to the shelter where he kept tools and such and grabbed a couple coils of rope, just in case he needed it.

Chapter 25

It took over an hour to get to the top of the game trail. He went as fast as he could travel in the snowshoes. The pup was with him the whole way.

He was actually starting to sweat a little, so he forced himself to slow down so as not to freeze when he stopped—if he stopped. If he got wet, the cold would eventually freeze his wet clothes and he wouldn't be any help to anybody after that. If there was anybody still alive.

Even still, he couldn't waste any time because anyone still alive would freeze in short order, especially if they were laying outside of the plane in the open. There was also the possibility of wolves or coyotes. Everything would be working against them. He needed to get there.

Upon reaching the top of the rock wall, he traveled east for maybe one hundred yards. He could see where the body of the plane slid in the snow heading for the timber at the lower end of the upper lake.

"Where was it?" he asked himself. Jogging down the slide left by the plane, he came to a large dip about fifty feet wide and twenty feet deep. This is where the plane had slid into and stopped. Almost hidden by snow and debris pushed up and over itself.

He slid down to the plane and dug the snow away from the door with his hands. He got the door open and found the pilot was alive, still strapped in the seat.

While unsnapping the safety belt, pulling him out of the seat and away from the plane, he came to the realization that it wasn't a man. It was a woman, and what was she doing flying on a night such as this?

The wind was blowing hard up here, and there was a crystal-like substance in the air, which was more ice than snow that felt like it was cutting the skin right off your face.

He knew he had to get her to shelter as quickly as possible, and looking around, he found a couple of small trees that had been broken off by the plane. Taking his knife out of its sheath, he chopped the ends off and cleaned all the limbs from the trees.

He sat these about two feet apart and wrapped the rope around them, making a travois for her to lay. This would at least hold her until he could get her to the cave at the bottom of the rocks. This was his first thought; he would get her to the cabin tomorrow, if possible.

When he started to pick up the end of the poles and drag her, the pup started whining. He looked around and saw him scratching at the door. What was the matter? There was no one else in the plane, or so he thought. He had looked in the back seat when he first opened the door.

He opened the door back up and saw nothing. Then he heard small voices whimpering on the floor between the front and back seat.

There, on the floor, were a bundle of quilts. He felt around and found a small child. When he tried to pull the child out, he found there was another child wrapped up in the quilts with this one.

They were both alive. *Unbelievable,* he thought. He couldn't tell if they were hurt or not, but they were crying and trying to kick the quilts off their small bodies.

One kept crying for mommy, and the other just cried hysterically. He talked to them while pulling the quilts apart enough to see for sure what all was there.

They looked to be okay; he could see no blood or cuts on the children, but there wasn't enough light to see that well in the plane.

They quieted a little as Steve spoke to them, then the bigger one asked for her mommy. He told them she was okay but couldn't talk right now, and he would take them to her.

He rewrapped the children and took them from the plane. He placed them on their mom's chest and tied them to her.

The two children were still warm from being cuddled together in the quilts, plus the fact that the quilts had obviously cushioned them from anything they might have bounced against because they didn't seem to be hurt. He'd have to come back after the rest of their stuff later.

Picking up the poles and wrapping the rope around his chest and shoulders, he started toward the trail, down off the high wall. That was his next worry: getting everybody down safely.

When he got to the wall, he rested a few minutes. He was tired and wet from sweating. He couldn't rest long or fear of freezing himself, and he wouldn't be any help to anyone that way. Besides, he knew he had to get to the cave. It was dry in there, and there was enough wood for at least a week, if need be.

He wrapped one end of his longest rope around a tree and tied it securely to the woman before taking the children from her. Then he slid the travois over the edge of the high wall, letting it down as slowly as possible.

Once it was on the ground, he threw the remainder of the rope over and out a ways, so it wouldn't land on the woman.

Using the remainder of his ropes, he tied the children up in the quilts, so they couldn't fall out, and strapped them to his back before starting down.

Once at the bottom, he ran over to the woman and turned her upright. Then, dragging her to the cave as quickly as possible, he pulled the blankets off of her face and head to see if she was okay. Still out, but okay.

He lit the lamp, then wrapped her and the children all together, thinking to himself how glad he was that the pup had been there. He'd have left the children there to freeze just as sure as anything.

Starting a fire, he watched as the smoke went out of an opening at the top of the cave. The wood was dry and made little smoke, but he didn't need smoke in his lungs or anyone else's, especially the children or the woman.

Then he took off his inner clothes and placed them over a ledge that was close to the fire to dry. He had to get them dry as quickly as possible, so he wouldn't get chilled himself.

The rock walls were starting to warm up now, and the little cave was actually getting comfortable.

His clothes were dry in just a little while. He got dressed and then pulled the blankets off the woman and the children. They were okay and started waking up as soon as they were uncovered.

Other than a big knot on the woman's head and a couple of small cuts, she seemed to be okay. The biggest cut was on top of her head and would never show should there be any kind of a scar that would amount to anything.

She'd have some bad bruises, though, and she still wasn't conscious. This worried him a little, but her breathing was normal, and her pulse seemed strong to him.

Taking her coat off so all three could lay together and share the body heat, he covered them with the quilts and added wood to the fire before laying back against the cave wall to rest himself.

The last thing he remembered was the pup slipping in under the canvas, which he had stretched across the opening of the cave and laying down. He laid right there at the opening as if to say, 'Go ahead and rest; I'll be right here.'

Chapter 26

Hearing the pup growl, he opened one eye. The woman was trying to reach over and pull the pistol from its holster.

"Lady, that's not a good idea. Your hand probably won't work right for a while, and I won't stop the pup from grabbing it."

She backed away with a look in her eyes that could kill. She sat back down beside the children and turned toward the fire.

He didn't know if the pup would have grabbed her or not, but it sounded good, and she sure changed her mind quickly enough.

"Lady, I spent most of the night saving you and your children's lives, so you could at least be a little more appreciative."

"I wasn't going to hurt you," she said after a long silence. "I just need to keep moving."

Steve let that lay for the time being. He got up and asked the children if they were hungry. They were scared and half-crying, so he squatted down in front of them and as softly as he could, he told them he wasn't going to hurt them, and if they were hungry, he would fix them something.

They looked at their mom, and she nodded her head, meaning that it would be okay. The little girl of about three, he guessed, looked at him and mumbled, "Yes, please."

He walked over to the rock shelf, grabbed a pan, and unpacked it. He rinsed it off in the spring-fed low spot in the rock, which held maybe a gallon of water before running out through another crack in the rocks and disappearing.

He opened a can of soup and poured it and some water in the pan. Then he placed the pan on some coals and stirred the soup until it was warm. Placing it in cups, he then handed it to the children.

He told the woman that when they were finished, she could have whatever was left. He threw that in just for effect; he didn't like the way she was acting, so he figured he'd put her in her place right off the bat.

Then he told her he was going back to the plane to get the rest of her things. He'd be back in an hour or so and then he'd take them to the cabin. "Be ready to go" was the last thing he said as he walked through the canvas door and out the opening.

At the plane, he grabbed two, big suitcases and a large duffel bag. That was pretty much everything he could find. Grabbing limbs and tree branches and what brush he could tear up, and what the plane had uprooted, he proceeded to cover the plane as completely as possible. He didn't know why, but he sensed the woman did not want to be found. He would know more later.

Walking back to where the wings had been ripped off, he could see that they were laying edge ways between the rocks and were mostly hidden by debris, other than the one that was sticking up a little, which was catching a reflection off the moon the night before.

Jerking it down, he finished covering it with tree limbs making it almost impossible to see, and after a little more brush, it was hidden completely.

He knew the woman wanted to keep on moving, and he really didn't want anyone finding his valley anyway, so he really didn't figure she'd care if he hid everything anyway.

When he got to the bottom of the trail, he saw her standing out from the cave, looking around. He told her there was nowhere to go, and she turned around so fast that she slipped and fell.

Picking herself up as fast as possible, she told him, "I thought you'd be back in an hour." He looked at her and told her he'd taken the time to hide the wreckage.

She looked at him for a second before saying, "Thank you." Then she followed him into the cave.

"Figured as much" was all that was said as he walked on in. He saw where she had cleaned and repacked everything.

He walked back out and gathered up his rope and the Travis he had made. "How'd you get us off that cliff?"

"I carried the children on my back." That was all that he said.

She looked at the rope he was rolling up and backup the vertical wall. Then she shuddered and very quietly said, "I'm glad I missed that."

He tied everything to the Travis and then placed the children on it. Lifting it, he wrapped the rope over his shoulders and started dragging everything toward the cabin.

The pup went ahead, and the woman followed.

"We have to hurry; there's a big storm blowing in, and it'll probably beat us to the cabin. Are you going to be able to make it?"

"Don't look back; please, just get the children there."

By the time he got the children to the cabin, the storm was on them. The wind wasn't bad yet, but the snowflakes were as big as a quarter and falling so hard you could hear them hitting the ground.

He looked around and she wasn't there. *Damn it, she was there just a minute ago*, he thought. *I hope the hell she just sat down exhausted and was not blundering around trying to find her way.* How'd she get off his trail anyway?

He packed the children up to the cabin as fast as possible and opened the vent and damper on the stove after placing them on the bed. They were sleepy anyway, so he made sure they were covered and put wood in the stove.

There were only a few coals left, so he had to put some very dry kindling in first. The cabin wasn't really warm, but it wasn't freezing, either.

Running back out and down the trail he had left, which was filling with snow fast, he told himself he should have tied a rope to her. He knew he had but little time to find her.

He saw where she had veered off for some reason, and he hollered. He heard nothing but the snow hitting the ground. He had little time left to find her, and the visibility was only about ten feet at most. He hollered again, and this time, he heard the pup bark not far from him.

It ran up to him and then turned and went straight back in the direction it had come. He followed for about fifty feet before he found her, just sitting there.

"What do you think you're trying to do?"

"I was trying to think things through when I realized I wasn't on the trail anymore. So, I just sat down instead of running around looking everywhere, hoping I wasn't too far from the trail and that you would come back and find me. The pup came up to me and laid down beside me, so I was hoping that if you got close, he'd bark or something."

"Good thinking," was all he said, and helped her up and headed for the cabin. He had very little tracks to follow by now, but enough to find the west wall, and then he worked his way around to the steps that went up to the cabin.

The pup went ahead of them for the last fifty yards or so, and he had those tracks to follow more than anything. Getting up to the cabin, he let her in and checked the fire. It was blazing, so he shut the damper back.

It was already warm inside. He went back out and put everything away. Then he brought the suitcases, quilts, and duffel bag up to the cabin. She had the coats off herself and the children when he got back inside. He showed her where she could get cleaned up and started fixing something to eat.

"Here's the first aid kit," he told her. "Anything you need help with, let me know. Other than the cut on your head, I didn't see anything seriously wrong with you."

Chapter 27

The next morning, he told her he couldn't believe how lucky everyone had been; how the body of the plane had went between the split in the rocks perfectly stripping the wings from the plane and how the landing gear had been torn off from the top of the rock wall.

"That must have been when you hit your head and the children had come off the seat and hit on the floor of the plane between the front and rear seat." The body of the plane just kept on sliding on top the snow, until the brush and small trees had slowed it enough that when it went into the small ravine, it had just gently stopped at the bottom.

All this was said while he was fixing breakfast for everyone. He told the woman that she must've had one hell of a good reason for flying in weather like that, and when she didn't say anything, he let it drop. He guessed she had her reasons.

He went out and fed the pup, and when he came back in, he was carrying an armload of wood. He placed it in the wood box before going back into the cave and up onto the ledge above the cabin.

Everything was white, about a foot of it. He went back down and started cleaning up after breakfast. The woman started helping, and together, they were finished pretty quickly.

After everything was cleaned up, she finally spoke her first words since the night before. "I want to thank you," she told him. "We'll be gone as soon as possible. As soon as the roads are clear, I will pay you to take me to an airport and for all your trouble."

"Follow me," he told her, walking into the cave and back up to the shelf above the cabin. Walking out, he told her to look carefully around. Looking around for a minute, she finally asked what his point was.

"Do you see any roads out of here?"

"No."

"Exactly; there aren't any."

"I have to go."

"You can't."

"They will find me."

"Not before spring they won't, not unless they had a radar fixed on your plane or a tracking device, of sorts. Now start talking. What am I in for? Who's they, and what's going on? I wouldn't ask, but it looks like it's going to become my business."

"I became mixed up with the wrong person a few years back. I thought I loved the man, but soon realized what he was. He is a drug runner and a killer. I started paying attention when I accidentally saw him kill a man for no reason whatsoever; he just shot him."

"I was able to get back to the back of the house without anyone seeing me, and when he found me, I was with the children. I just smiled and played with the children, acting as if nothing was wrong whatsoever. It must have worked because he said nothing to me about anything.

"That was about three months ago. A few days ago, I heard him talking to one of his buddies, and I overheard him say that it was time for me to disappear. So, I gathered up what belongings I could without being noticed and hid them where I could get to them easily.

"He left for some kind of meeting, and I took my suitcases out and hid them in the hanger where he keeps his private jet. As quickly as I could get back, I gathered up the children, what blankets and quilts I could carry, and snuck out.

"He didn't know that I could fly, and I'm glad I never mentioned it to him. I knew the weather was turning bad, but I had no choice. It's all history now, and I guess you deserve to know. You're probably right in the middle of something you don't want or need to be in now, and I'm sorry. I truly am."

Steve listened without saying anything. When she was finished, he thought for a second, then told her not a lot could be changed now, so they'd make the best of the situation.

"Check your bags for anything that might have any kind of sending unit or anything like that it." He doubted it, but he wanted to cover all the bases. *Can't be too careful*, he thought.

They went in and back down to the children. They were playing on the bearskin rug, which he had put on the floor.

"Check everything now," he said. "I'm going to go check the plane for any kind of tracking device while the weather is holding."

They looked through her bags and found nothing, which is what he figured she'd find.

"I see nothing at all."

"Did you check everything?"

"Yes."

"How about that big duffel bag?"

"That's not mine."

"It was in the plane. See what's in it."

She opened it and turned a pale white. She just sat down looking kind of sick.

"What is it?"

"Look."

He opened the bag and looked. It was full of money. Stacks of hundred-dollar bills with a nine-millimeter, semi-automatic pistol lying on top.

It was a large bag, and he had no idea how much was in it. He emptied it out on the bed and checked for any kind of sending device. There was nothing in the money, but checking the bag over thoroughly, he found an outside pocket just below the strap handle. He unzipped the pocket, taking out a small sending unit. It was on.

Looking it over, he found a little switch and pushed it to the off position. The little red light went off. He took the box apart, removed the little battery, and then he threw everything in the stove.

"I don't know anything about these things, but hopefully he didn't have any kind of a fix on you. Maybe he could just follow a homing device of sorts to locate the money."

She looked up at him with tears in her eyes and said, "I'm sorry. I don't know what else to say."

"Nothing can be said or done now."

"He'll kill you, even if I'm not here. He won't believe you don't know anything, and he'll kill you. Even if he's convinced you don't know."

"I might not die so easily. Especially since I know he's coming."

"How would you know?"

"If he's close, the pup will tell me. The only way to get in here now is by helicopter, and we'll hear that."

"Come outside a second." They stepped out on the ledge, under the overhang.

"He can't see the cabin unless he's right in front of it. From above, it can't be seen; everything is pretty much hidden."

"Now, do you see the split in the rocks on top of the main wall? Just ahead the main wall goes back into another valley."

"I don't know exactly where you're talking about."

"Look at the end of the lake."

"Okay."

"Now, in a straight line from you, look at the high wall."

"Do you mean the cliff?"

"Yes! I've always called them high walls. Don't know why just have, I guess."

"Okay, now what?"

"At the top, do you see where the rock splits into two pieces like an opening or something? Just a space between two big rocks."

"Yes, I see where you're talking about."

"That's where your plane went through."

"What?"

"You threaded it like a needle. That's how lucky you were. The moon reflected its light off the wings as they folded back and were ripped off the plane. Your running gear hit the high wall and fell to the bottom. God had to have been with you as copilot last night. I really don't see how anyone could have been that lucky."

"I don't know about God, but I believe something was helping me because I had no control of the plane when the cross wind hit me like it did. The plane was doing whatever it wanted, and I remember being slammed against the windshield or something, and that's all."

"That doesn't matter now. Look to the left of the two rocks that the plane went through."

"Okay."

"It's hard to see, but there's a little ledge that comes down into the valley."

"I don't see it."

"You'll be able to when you know exactly where it is."

"Okay, what's your point?"

"I'll be going over there in an hour or so if I can get over. If they come in the valley, that's the only way in from the wreckage. If you see me go over, you'll know where it is. We'll need to keep our eyes on that game trail, and maybe we'll see them coming in, if we're lucky."

"What makes you think we'll get that lucky?"

"The pup will know, or one of the other animals will. You'll learn to notice if a horse, moose, elk, or any of the animals in this valley happen to look that way, and believe me, they will. You just have to learn to see what you're looking at, so to speak."

The pup was lying by the woodpile, just watching them. Steve told the woman he was going back in, but before she came back in to grab a piece of dried meat out of the cabinet and throw it over close to the dog. "Don't try to pet him or anything. Let him make up to you; he will soon enough."

Inside he grabbed his rifle and pistol before stepping back out. Then he strapped on his snowshoes, telling her that within about an hour, to start watching for him at the high wall.

It shouldn't take more than an hour and a half for him to get to the top, and then she'd know where the trail was.

"When weather is better, I'll show you the other trails in and out of here. As soon as I can, I will help you and the children get safely away."

"Thank you so much."

"Do you know how to use a pistol?"

"Yes, very well, thanks."

"Then keep the nine-millimeter on your belt; it should make you feel better. If you think you need to lock the door, just pull the rope back through the hole. That lifts the plank up out of the hook. Simple as that."

"I think I can figure that out." She smiled.

"Sometimes I talk more than I need to. I didn't mean anything by it."

"It's all right. I didn't take offense, and I appreciate everything you've done."

Chapter 28

It took a good hour for him to get to the trail up. The going was slow because of the drifting snow.

Finally making it, he studied the trail as best he could before heading up. It looked like he would have a hard time getting up, but also he felt like he had to, if possible.

It was probably too late, but for the children and her safety, he had to try. Plus, his own personal reasons of not wanting anyone finding his home.

It took a good half hour to make his way to the top. He had to kick the snow off most of the trail as he made his way up to the top.

Making the top, he rested for a few minutes while looking everything over. He could see where he had crossed the valley and also knew the trail wouldn't be visible for very long with the weather being like it was.

Looking ahead, he saw a small pack of wolves on the opposite side of the lake, working their way into the timber on the upper side. He watched as they weaved in and out of the trees and finally dropped out of sight over a little knoll, which went in behind some rocks.

After a minute, he headed in the direction of the plane. He looked for anything that might be sending a signal, but he found nothing. The plane was well-hidden, but he thought he better do a better job of it.

He checked the fuel in the plane and thought that there was more than enough to blow the plane up, if he was lucky. He wasn't sure it would work, but he thought he would try anyway.

Taking his knife, he punched a hole in the tank about halfway down, letting the fuel run out onto the rocks and the snow below.

It ran straight down the ravine, toward the timber. He could see the snow melting as it ran down toward the bottom. Then he walked on down a safe distance away and waited.

He could see and smell the fuel before it got there, so he knew exactly where it was going to empty into the ditch. Digging the snow away until he could see the frozen ground and grass, he waited for it to arrive.

In just a little while, the grass was wet with fuel, so he lit a match and dropped it. The fuel ignited, and he could hear and see the flames run up the bank, straight for the plane. The melting snow made a slight sizzle as the fire made its way up over the bank to its destination.

Within a few seconds of lighting the fire, the plane burst into flames with a loud explosion.

At first, he thought he might not have been far enough away. He had no idea the explosion would have been so great.

He jumped behind a rock and laid there until everything quieted down. The fire and smoke must have gone one hundred feet in the air, with pieces of plane flying everywhere.

He walked back to the plane, picking up pieces of debris as he went. He spent the bigger part of the day throwing everything back on the fire.

Everything that would burn finally did, and what was left he covered with brush. The snow was melted in at least a fifty-foot radius around the plane when the fire was finally out. Then he gathered everything up and threw it on what was left of the plane before covering it.

The snow should have everything covered by morning, and when the weather broke, he'd come back up and do a better job of hiding everything, but this would have to do until then.

He headed back in and could see there was another storm on the way. That was a good thing; now he was sure that everything would be covered by morning and probably well before.

He got back to the cabin a little after dark and fed the pup before going in. The pup hadn't left his side all day. Even when they had watched the small pack of wolves cross the upper meadow, he hadn't shown any signs of wanting to leave his side.

He stepped inside the cabin and was surprised when he saw his supper was waiting for him.

"I saw you coming off the wall and tried to time it, so you would have a hot meal when you got here."

"I appreciate it."

"I saw the plane blow; did you find anything?"

"No, I tried to destroy everything, then cover up anything that wouldn't burn. I'll have to do a better job when the weather breaks."

"Thank you so much."

"It's okay; it's in everyone's best interest. I wouldn't want anything to happen to a couple of innocent children, and I really don't think you deserve to be killed, either. I don't know you very well, but I don't think you're lying to me."

"I've told you the truth. I'd been noticing little things over the last couple of years, and I knew things were getting bad for me, but I had no idea they were that bad."

"Thanks again for supper, it was delicious."

"You're welcome; it's the very least I can do."

With that, she started cleaning the dishes. There was only his, so he went ahead and started cleaning his rifle.

She brought them both a hot cup of coffee and sat down at the table across from him.

"Did you have to use that today?"

"No, but it was in the weather all day, and I clean them both every night. Do you know anything about guns?"

"Enough, I guess. I'm a fair shot, but never had to clean them. Someone else always did that for me."

"Grab the pistol, and I'll show you. You're going to need to know how to do this, and I'll show you how to clean the rifle next time. Out here, these can be your best friend, and you need to treat them as such. This way they'll never let you down."

He took the time to teach her how to load and unload the gun first. Then, how to take it apart and clean it. She learned quickly, and after several times, she could take it apart and put it back together almost as quickly as he could.

"My guns are always loaded, so treat them as such after tonight. I'll be sure and keep them up out of reach of the children, but if they even look like they want to touch them, you crack their fingers or behind and tell them not to touch them.

"No matter where the guns are, I don't want to have to worry about the children, understand?"

She looked at him sort of funny and said nothing.

"I'm serious. A small slap on the backside now is a whole lot better than one of them getting shot. The recoil off one of these could hurt the child bad enough. No means no, and in this country, it's important that they know that."

The children had fallen asleep on the bearskin, so Steve got a blanket and covered them.

"You can have my bed; it's warmer out here anyway. I'll fix up that little side room for myself tomorrow. I'll sleep in the cave tonight."

Picking up his blanket, he walked back to the cot in the cave, leaving the door open so as to leave some of the heat back in.

Chapter 29

The next morning, he awoke early, feeling half-frozen. He damn sure was going to finish cleaning out that little side room in the cabin, and he was going to start first thing after breakfast.

There was mostly leftover pipe, fittings, ropes, boots, etc. Nothing that couldn't be in the cave for now, anyway.

Obviously, over the years, it had been turned into a catch-all, so to speak. A lot of it was just extra clothes and coats, which could remain in there but had to be folded and placed on shelves or hung up instead of just thrown on the bed.

He got up and went out into the main room of the cabin. Everyone else was still snuggled up in their beds and asleep. It was getting a little cool in there also, so he opened the stove up and stirred the coals.

Throwing some smaller sticks of dry wood on the coals, he watched them light almost immediately. Then he added wood and closed the door, leaving the drafts open.

He put water in the coffee pot and placed it on the stove. It wasn't long before the stove was hot and the room was warming up. The coffee was starting to perk, so he just sat back and waited.

Looking over, he noticed the woman was watching him.

"Coffee will be done in a few minutes."

"It smells good."

"It gets you going in the mornings."

He poured two cups, and she got up and sat down at the table, putting both hands around the cup and allowing that to help warm her fingers. She sipped at the coffee and looked up at him.

"You're right; it does wake you up. It kind of wakes your whole body up as that first sip goes down."

"I enjoy sitting here while the sun comes up and drinking a pot in the mornings."

"What? The sun hasn't come up yet?"

"Not for another half hour or so."

"What time is it?"

"Don't know for sure; don't have a watch."

"Guess, please."

"Maybe six-thirty. It gets light a little later here in the valley, then on top. It just takes a little longer for the sun to pop over the high wall. If you look out, you can see the sun coming over the top of the mountain, though. It won't be long, and you'll be able to feel it. It'll actually shine on the front of the cabin and still be a dark shadow back toward the east wall."

"Another time."

"It's nice in the spring and summer. You'll like it."

"I won't be here."

"You'll see some of the spring weather before the snow melts and we'll be able to get you out."

"I'll leave as soon as possible. I'm sure you'll be tired of me and the children by then anyway."

"We'll make do. I'll spend as much time outside as weather permits. If you want, you can take the children out, too. Just watch the ledge, it's a good twenty feet down. It slopes some at the bottom, but you still don't want to fall off."

The children were starting to stir, so he got up and went back to the cave. He brought back a slab of smoked side meat and sliced off some bacon. While the bacon was frying, she mixed up some pancakes. Twenty minutes later, breakfast was on the table. The children ate like they were starved. She couldn't believe it. "I've never seen them eat like that."

Sipping his coffee, he looked up at her and said, "The food was pretty good, and there is something about the mountains that makes one's appetite a little crazy."

"Yes, I agree. I'll have to watch, or I'll get fat. Especially if there's nothing to do but sit in here."

"There's plenty to do; only if you feel like sitting in here you can. There's always tomorrow. I guess you could say it's kind of laid-back here."

"If you don't mind me asking, don't you get bored here all alone?"

"This is my first winter here. The place belonged to someone else. He got too old to stay here and came to Ohio where we met. He gave me the place in exchange for a place to spend out his last days close to his family. All I need to do is put his ashes in a place he has ready here in the valley when he dies. Small price to pay for such a beautiful place."

"Is that all?"

"No, I just have to keep it clean where he can see the valley from that spot. Enough about me. Are the children asking about their dad?"

"No. Whenever he was around them, he was almost mean to them. He paid little attention to them. They got to where they'd hide from him when he was close or just hang on to me and try to keep me between themselves and him. They already act better around you. At least they don't seem to be afraid of you."

"How old are they?"

"She is four and he is three. They both just had birthdays a couple of weeks ago."

"I assume you had parties for them?"

"As much as possible."

"If you'd like, you can make a cake for them, we'll try to make it as happy a day as possible for them."

"Maybe, that would be nice." She looked at him with questions in her eyes.

"I'm not all that mean."

"The way you acted last night, I wasn't sure."

"Listen, it's very important they listen in this country. Inside or outside of this cabin, if they ignore you when you tell them something, especially when you tell them to or not to do something, it could be very bad or even fatal. I know that sounds a little extreme, but it's not."

"I'll try to understand and do as you ask while we're here."

"I'm serious. I hardly know these kids, but I would have a hard time living with myself if I let something happen to them. Especially something I could have stopped. I'll only be asking for them to listen to me while they are here. Fair enough?"

"Fair enough."

"I haven't asked yet, but what are their names?"

"Anna and Shane."

"And yours?"

"It's Tonya; are you going to tell me yours?"

"Just plain old Steve. Glad to meet you."

"The pleasure's all mine."

"Okay, now I have to get that side room cleaned out. I'm not sleeping in that cave another night."

Chapter 30

After cleaning the side bedroom, he started building two, small beds for the children. They seemed excited about having their own bed, so he let them help as much as they could without getting hurt.

They had plenty of time because the weather wasn't improving any. Mostly they were in the way, but he showed them all the patience in the world.

Tonya asked once if the children were bothering him. He just looked at her for a second before asking, "Why would they be? It's not like I'm in a big hurry to get anywhere."

Smiling, she just went on with whatever it was she was doing.

For the most part, Shane stayed close to his mother. He acted as if he was afraid that he'd be hollered at every time he picked something up or offered to help.

At first, Anna acted the same way, but quickly saw a soft spot in Steve and took advantage. It got to whenever he would growl at her, she would just look up at him with her big, dark eyes, and make a face and growl back. He would just grin at her, and it quickly became a game. It wasn't long before Shane played, too, but not as enthusiastically as Anna would.

Tonya was making cookies one afternoon and when she wasn't looking, and Steve grabbed two, giving them to the children. He held his finger up to his lips with a "shh." They both turned their backs to their mom and tried to hide their cookies while they ate them. About that time, Steve felt a small fist hit him in the middle of the back. Not that hard but still hard enough to get his attention. When he looked around, she just pointed her finger at him and went back to what she was doing. He could have sworn he had seen a slight grin on her face, though, and asked her what her problem was.

"No problem at all," was all that she said. She never looked back around at him.

As the day went on, he noticed her watching him out of the corner of her eye.

"Don't worry, I won't do it again."

"It's really okay. I'm just not used to anyone being nice to the children, or myself, for that matter. I hit you playing, really not knowing how else to react to your kindness. Please don't take it wrong."

With that, he noticed her eyes turned a little red just before she turned away from him. He went back to work on the beds, and a little later, without even looking up, he told her, "I didn't take it wrong, and I'm really sorry you were all treated so badly."

Chapter 31

It took the better part of a week for him to finish the two beds. During this time, he noticed how the woman's features were softening more every day.

She smiled a lot more and just looked a lot nicer. In fact, she was just plain easy to look at, and he liked having her and the children around, even though it was getting boring inside the cabin every day.

Finally, the weather broke enough that they could get out. He asked her if her and the children were up for a little adventure.

"Absolutely," was all that was said. She started grabbing clothes while he looked for boots and snowshoes. He had modified a pair for Tonya a few days before and had fixed up a small sleigh to pull the children on. He had covered the sides with canvas to make them airtight; plus, he had left enough extra hang over to make a cover, if necessary.

Every day he went out and kept the steps clear of snow, so as to be able to get them off of the ledge whenever the weather broke enough to get out for a while. When they were all out and off the ledge, he handed her the rifle and told her to stay close, just in case.

She had been getting very handy at handling the rifle. He had her clean it every night and had shown her how to use it, all without it being loaded.

Every day she practiced handling it, and she always acted as if it were loaded. She practiced loading and unloading it safely

When he handed it to her, all he said was, "It's ready." She hooked the sling over her head and one shoulder with the rifle on her back, barrel up as he had shown her. He had the pistol strapped around his waist and picked up the strap that was hooked to the sleigh.

"Where are we going?"

"To see how the horses are doing; if we can get there, that is."

"I brought some sandwiches in case we need them."

"Good. We'll build a fire somewhere and have a little picnic, if we can. I hope you brought some of those cookies you're so proud of."

"What do you mean?"

"You know! The ones you were ready to fight over."

She just smiled and made a face at him. Pulling the sleigh, they started across the valley toward the side fields where the horses usually stayed. He hollered for the pup, and it wasn't but a couple of minutes before it showed up.

Anna asked him what his name was.

"I just call him pup. He answers to that."

"That's not a very good name. I think I'll call him something else."

"What's wrong with pup?'

"I don't like it."

"Well, I do."

She made a face, then growled at him.

He just kind of chuckled and kept moving toward the opening of the field. Upon arriving at first, he saw nothing. Studying hard up under all the overhangs, he finally saw them. They

looked pretty good, and he could see where they'd been out palling up the alfalfa and clover, so he knew they were okay.

Then they went up under one of the overhangs, and he built a small fire. The children busied themselves gathering wood while Steve got some small sticks. After they got a fire going, he took some longer sticks that had a fork on one end and placed a sandwich on the fork, then held it over the fire. He handed Tonya another stick, and she did likewise. After a minute, they

turned the sandwich and held it back over the fire.

"How did you know to put cheese on the sandwiches?"

"I didn't; it was just the fastest and easiest."

"Well, it will make a perfect sandwich. I like grilled cheese."

"We do, too."

"Who said you two were getting any of my sandwiches?"

They looked at him for a second, then came the face. She growled at him and then smiled. He shook his head and smiled up at the Tonya. She smiled back and told him that he had created the little monster. They both grinned, and he handed both children half a sandwich.

After they had eaten, he watched as the horses worked their way out into the field and started grazing. Out in the field, he could see they were looking very well, so he sure wasn't going to worry about them today.

"If they start to lose a lot of weight, I'll start feeding them corn, but not until I have to. I want to make sure I have enough for the winter."

About that time, he noticed a wolf along the far wall walking along in a half-crouch. Pointing it out, they both watched for a while.

"What's it doing?"

"It's stocking something, but I can't see what."

"I see it; about one hundred feet ahead, there's a deer. It just jumped up out of its bed, and it's trying to run. It looks like it has a broken leg."

"It looks like the wolf has a limp itself. Give me the rifle."

"What are you going to do?"

"I'm not going to let the deer suffer."

"What about the wolf?"

"She and I go way back."

"What do you mean?"

"She's the pup's mom. She only has half of her right front foot. I'll tell you all about it later."

The wolf closed the distance within a matter of seconds. When the deer tried to spin away, the wolf grabbed her by the throat, pulling her to the ground and holding her there.

"I guess she's doing all right for herself," he said, and handed the rifle back to Tonya.

"We better get started back." He put out the fire and placed the children into the sleigh. The wind was picking up a little, so he fastened the canvas over top of them, making them the perfect, little shelter.

They stayed warm and out of the wind, wrapped in their quilts, and never complained once.

They got back to the cabin just before dark. The children were asleep, so he picked up the boy first and took him up to the cabin and laid him on his bed. When he got back down to the sleigh, she told him that the pup stood right against the sleigh and didn't move until he had come back into site from the split in the rock. "He didn't move until then."

"I guess he's made up to you and the children now, so you shouldn't have to worry about anything slipping up unexpected on you now. He'll let you know in a hurry and probably give his life for the children and most likely you, also."

Later that evening, Shane got up on his mother's lap and went to sleep. That wasn't a surprise, but it was a surprise when Anna crawled up on Steve's lap, curled up, and also went to sleep in seconds. Tonya said nothing; she just looked all warm and happy. She smiled and listened to the story as he told about mouse, pup, and his brother and two sisters.

"So, you were going to kill the deer just to make sure she had something to eat?"

"It had a broken leg. I'd have killed it anyway."

"I guess so."

After a while, he got up and put Anna to bed, and then he took the boy from his mother and carried him to his bed, also. She followed him over and made sure both children were tucked in nice and snug.

As Steve was loading up the stove, she kissed them both good night.

He got up from the stove and headed for his bed, saying good night as he went.

"Thank you."

"For what?"

"A wonderful day."

"You're welcome."

Chapter 32

Steve laid down and gradually felt his body warm and relax under the quilts. He was asleep in the matter of minutes. It was a sound sleep from being out in the weather all day, plus the fact that he'd pulled the sleigh behind him. He hadn't realized how tired he was until he got cleaned up and his stomach was full.

As he had told the story of the wolf, he had had a hard time staying awake. He had gone into great detail about Mouse and how the wolf had gradually made up to him. He described the fight with the bear and how the pups blood trail had led to mouse and his the rest of the pups.

She had asked if he would take her there one day, and he agreed to do so in the spring. He wanted to make sure that the plane was hidden anyway after the snow had melted. As soon as the grass and brush grew back, there shouldn't be any more problems keeping the plane hidden… or at least he hoped not.

As morning neared, he dreamed of the day when he had killed the bear and the fight that took place. A mad grizzly was as vicious as any creature he had ever seen. The dog and wolf were working as a team, keeping the bear off each other. In and out, they were grabbing and letting go.

The dream was in color; one of those rare dreams that was so vivid it was like it was happening all over again.

He was reloading his rifle and even saying how he'd like to kick the man's ass that made the law that a magnum rifle could only hold three rounds at a time.

He dreamed everything right up to the point of the bear collapsing as it charged at him, then about walking up and shooting it in the head with the pistol. He was trying to reload the pistol when he felt the presence of somebody in his room.

Not moving a muscle, he opened his eyes. It was pitch black, and he could see nothing, but he knew someone was there.

He quietly eased his hand over for the knife on his bedpost. The pistol was on Tonya's bedpost. How had they gotten past her without waking her? For that matter, how had they gotten in the cabin without making any noise or without the pup letting them know? They must have forgotten to pull the drawl rope out of the door, and obviously the pup had slipped off somewhere.

As he started to pull the knife, he heard a soft voice asking, "Are you awake? I could hear you mumbling something in your sleep."

"Yes, I guess I was dreaming."

As he answered her, he felt the covers pull back, and she sat down on the bed beside him.

"Dreaming about what?"

"The day the dogs and I killed the bear, is all."

As she asked, she pulled her legs up and slid under the covers next to him. She snuggled up against him, and he could feel she had nothing on. Her warm, soft body felt like heaven. This was the last thing he had expected; she was a lot younger and so very beautiful.

They made love until the sun came up, and afterward, they just lay there, not saying anything; each in their own thoughts, just holding on to each other.

"Sorry I woke you."

"I'm not." He pulled her close, and she folded herself back into his arms. He kissed her between her neck and shoulder and held her tight until they heard the children wake up and start to complain about the cabin being a little cold.

Chapter 33

The rest of the winter was like that mostly. They lived like a family, but he knew in his mind it couldn't last. In the same instance, it was wonderful, for now. The woman was so beautiful and full of life.

The children seemed to adore him as he did them.

They were outside doing whatever they could when the weather permitted. It was very seldom he went without them, even to hunt, unless the weather looked to get bad before the day was over. They had plenty of canned food and such, but he also tried to keep fresh meat on hand, also. Plus, the fact that sitting in the cabin was just plain boring at times.

He taught all three how to track and read signs, while Tonya taught the children how to read, do arithmetic, and such. They studied mostly when the weather was bad, or in the evenings when Steve didn't have them helping him through the day.

Shane did very well for three and could actually read a little when you could keep him still long enough to concentrate. At their ages, they both did very well, though, and Tonya never pushed them.

They both loved the outdoors and picked up on tracking very fast. They could tell which way a rabbit was moving and had a pretty good idea as to how old the tracks were. They loved studying the tracks and trying to figure out how old they might be and such.

Steve started calling the girl Morning Dove or sometimes Dove and the boy, Little Bear. He told them that they were Indian names and they loved to be called by them; so much, in fact, that they would correct their mom whenever she would call them by their given names.

They would try to keep track of Sundays and read from the Bible on these days. They decided they'd always try to make that a day of rest, if at all possible. As for right now, though, most every day was a day of rest, except Steve would try to make a trip around the valley most every day, if possible, just to check for signs of anyone or anything unwanted coming in.

Tonya was always worried about the children's real father finding them. Being that they never found the tracking device until two days after the crash, it was always in the back of her mind, and also Steve's.

Steve watched the wildlife as much as anything, hoping they'd tell him if anything or anyone was in the valley, but so far everything was normal. He hadn't seen any signs of anything abnormal.

The biggest change was in the pup. He was never too far away, and when the woman and children went out, he would stay very close to them. As if he knew they would need more looking after then Steve would.

This pup had grown. He had to weigh well over one hundred pounds now. He was muscular and looked a lot like his dad, other than he had enough wolf features to make any man take notice. He was a beautiful animal in which a person would not want to have turn on him. It was springtime now, and even though it was still cool at night, the weather was warming up nicely through the day. He knew the pup wasn't finished growing, but he had no idea how much more filling out he would do.

Funny thing was he was always close by, just out of reach. Neither Steve or Tonya could pet the dog other than when he wanted petted, but the children could wrestle all over the dog, and he seemed to enjoy it. He was a perfect babysitter; nothing got close to the children, nor did the children get close to anything that might hurt them.

On more than one occasion, they saw him grab Little Bear by the arm and pull him away from the rock ledge, or other things that might have gotten him hurt.

The girl also would get upset at times when she couldn't do something because the dog wouldn't let her get close enough to somewhere she wanted to be.

For Steve, everything was perfect, but he sensed a change in Tonya as the snow melted and the weather got nicer. He told himself he knew it was too good to last anyway and come what may; it had been good while it lasted.

Chapter 34

As time passed, the days grew warmer and longer. He and the children had gotten closer. There would always be a warm feeling come over him whenever they were near. They would play with things for hours that he really couldn't understand how it would hold their interest for more than five minutes. Whenever he would tell them anything, the children would listen without question, which kept them from getting hurt on more than one occasion. Just little things that could have gone wrong but did not because they listened.

The best of it was when they would both crawl up on his lap and fall asleep before bedtime. He loved them dearly and knew it would be lonely when they left.

The woman seemed to drift farther and farther away. She was so quiet anymore, and he didn't know what to make of it, so one night he just put it straight to her asking what the problem was.

"Nothing. I have no problem."

"There's something; don't I have the right to know?"

"When can we leave?"

"The passes are open; never said you had to stay."

"That's the problem. You don't say anything."

"What do you want me to say? I'm fifty-one years old, you're thirty-six. You're anxious to leave, but you don't know where you can go, so you just keep hanging on."

"Is that how you feel?"

"I try not to feel a lot of anything. It's going to be lonely when you leave."

"Is it?"

"Yes; how could you think differently?"

"I thought you liked your solitude."

"I did, but you changed that."

"How's that?"

"How do you think?"

"I don't know, tell me."

"First off, there are the children. I love them dearly and it's not going to be easy starting the day off not telling them everything I'm doing or planning to do. I've gotten where I look forward to it. Also, explaining how something is done or why it's done in such a way. They're full of questions, and I guess I enjoy teaching them."

"I've noticed that. You're not like any man I've ever known. You always take the time for the children, and for me, for that matter. I'm not used to it."

"You want me to change?"

"No! I'm just confused, and I don't understand my feelings."

"What do you mean?"

"I mean you're fifteen years older than me, and I don't understand why I look at you and I can't even imagine being with anyone else. To be honest, the first time I came to your bed, it was a combination of things. You were kind to me and my children; a good man, or at least that was all I could see."

"And now?"

"I still feel the same way, other than I'm not lonely anymore, nor do I need a man. I have you. One more thing: at the time, I had no idea that you were fifteen years older than me. You don't look to be fifty-one years old."

"So, what are you trying to say?"

And then she covered her face and ran outside.

After a minute, he walked out behind her and placed a blanket over her shoulders before resting his hands there.

"That's what I'm talking about! You're thoughtful, on top of everything else. It's still a little cool in the evenings, and you thought of that before you came out."

"I just try to take care of the things and people I care about."

"You care about?"

"If you don't know that by the things I do for you by now, I guess you'll never figure it out."

She turned to him and put her arms around him, holding him tight. She said nothing for a while. Finally, without looking up but holding on with all of her being, she said, "I love you," and started crying.

He waited until she quit before saying anything himself. Then he pulled her chin up and looked into her eyes. "I love you, too," he said, and then he kissed her as gently as he possibly could.

They went back inside and went to bed.

Later, when she had her back to him and her body was formed tightly to his, holding onto his arms, which were wrapped firmly around her, she told him. "I'm very afraid of what's going to happen. I feel better and happier than I've ever felt in my life. Thank you for that."

"What else is on your mind?"

"I know that he is going to show up. There's a lot of money in that bag, and he's not going to give that up."

"I know, I've been thinking about that some. We'll talk on it tomorrow. We have to decide where to go and what the other is going to do in case we get separated; a place to meet, that sort of thing, but that's tomorrow."

She snuggled back into his arms even tighter and said one more time, "I love you."

He squeezed and told her that he loved her, too.

After a minute or two of silence, he chuckled.

"What?"

"If anything changes I'll let you know."

His reward for that remark was an elbow in the ribs. Then she shook her head, and a smile formed across her lips before she went to sleep feeling better than she had felt in her entire life.

Chapter 35

The next morning, Steve was up before daylight. He packed a backpack with enough food for the day and started breakfast. The coffee was perking when he felt her arms wrap around him from behind.

"Good morning."

"Good morning to you."

"What's up?"

"We're going for a walk."

"A walk?"

"Yes, it's time to prepare. Just in case. Wake the children."

Without another word, she woke the two, and by the time they'd all eaten, he had them excited about a picnic. This made the children very happy and excited about going on another little adventure.

"Where?"

"A surprise."

He grabbed the pack and rifle, placing the pistol belt around his waist. Then he handed the nine-millimeter to Tonya. They went out the back of the cabin and through the cave. Up on top, he showed her both trails telling her about the waterfall and the cave behind.

"There is no way to get off the ledge in that direction, unless you jump to one of the trees and climb down. That's the only way it can be done. I guess that would be easy enough if it has to be."

They went toward the cave, where the cougar had stayed. On top, he pointed out how the valley laid and approximately where the trails were in and out. From there, you could see where the plane had crashed over the wall and where the game trail was leading to the top. A person could also see the side valley and how it ran around to the north and back to the point where they now stood.

"It's beautiful."

"Keep it in your mind; you need to remember every trail and shelter. Maybe you won't, but when you see it again, you might. Once you have a picture in your mind of everything, you'll be able to remember easily enough as you see different things."

They started north, working their way around. They couldn't move very fast because of the children, but they did okay. The questions they asked would help Tonya remember, plus it would give her enough time to study the landmarks and such.

Early afternoon they stopped for the picnic he had promised.

"This is where I killed the grizzly."

"Right here?"

"Not exactly, this is the trail I ran down to get back to where the wolf and dog were fighting."

"Weren't you afraid?"

"Didn't have time to be afraid, but after it was all over, I shook some. I'm not going to lie to you about that. It was a rush, to say the least."

"Listen; I hear something."

"The pup probably; it took him long enough. I figured he'd find us an hour ago. Coming from that direction, there must be another way up that I haven't found yet. I'll look another day."

He made a small fire and heated their sandwiches. They ate, and the children took a nap. The pup laid down beside them, so he took her by the hand and led her to the location he had shot the bear from.

From here she could see the side valley and how it ran around and back to the point where they now stood.

"I haven't had time to look this over yet, but you can see how it lays. There's a game trail up here and probably another one or two leading around the north end of the valley. Do you think the children are up to it?"

"I don't know."

"Do you think we have enough food?"

"I packed plenty."

"Okay, then, we'll just take our time and camp for the night if we find a good shelter. We can always use the cave where we spent that first night. Now, see the ledge going around the wall about half way up?"

"Yes."

"Any trails up or down we'll find from there. I see nothing but timber on the top, and as long as a person skirts the top of the wall, they can't get lost. Let's get back."

"Just a second."

"What's wrong?"

"We haven't taken a minute for each other yet."

"This is all for us."

"Not what I mean."

Hugging him for a couple of seconds, she told him, "I'm happy now, let's go."

"Here or on that ledge?"

"For what?"

"To meet if something separates us."

"On the ledge."

They skirted the ledge around and found that it was plenty wide and flat enough to be safe for travel. He told the children to stay away from the edge, and they did so without question. Looking up at him, she said that she was sorry for ever questioning him that day when he told her they would listen without question. She understood the importance now.

"I'll never question you again on anything."

"It's okay; I'm not always right, but I have my reasons. You don't have to apologize. You wouldn't have understood at the time, and I knew that."

They found three more splits in the rocks that could be maneuvered to the top and one which had been heavily used by deer at different times. This one angled up toward the top and was about two feet wide.

There were only a couple of trails down. They didn't look to be that easily traveled but passable. There were several trees that reached above the ledge with lots of limbs. Worse came to worse, they could be reached and then a person could climb down, but not with the children.

They circled the side valley and made their way to the top. The ledge gradually climbed to the top about three hundred yards from where they had had lunch. Around the top, at the northern end of the valley, he came across a trail leading down a short distance and ending at a small cave. Actually, it was just an overhang that went back in. There was plenty of shelter from the weather, but only one way in and out.

"We'll stay here. I'll gather some wood for a fire while you unpack everything."

He started the fire, and they ate their fill. They had hot soup and sugar-cured ham, along with homemade biscuits. There was water for the little ones, and the two of them sat back and drank coffee.

He tucked the children back between the fire and the rock wall, which was soaking up the heat, making it perfect for the children to sleep.

The two of them curled up together on the opposite side of the fire after he positioned himself, so he could keep wood on the fire without waking anyone. The pup laid down beside the fire, facing the children, and never moved.

Chapter 36

The next morning, they woke early, and after breakfast, they walked around the north end of the main valley. The food was gone, so he made the pack work for Shane to ride on his back when he got too tired to walk. Anna wanted to walk, and the trail was open, so they still made good time around to the game trail that led down.

"Where are we now?"

"This is where I lowered you down off the cliff."

"Have I told you how glad I am that I missed that?"

"Maybe once or twice."

"Just thought I might mention it again."

"You're just lucky I was in a good mood."

"I'm glad you were."

"It wouldn't have made any difference now, over there is where the remains of your plane are."

"Okay, they seem to be well-hidden."

"They are; from here, anyway."

"At the end of that little lake, the water runs into a stream and flows over the wall about fifty feet into a pool of water. A person could jump in if they needed to. The water is plenty deep enough. Then you're in the side valley where the horses are."

"It's beautiful up here."

"Yes, it is, in the fall, especially. I've seen moose, elk, and deer a plenty here; also, a few wolves."

"Where's Mouse buried?"

"Look up at the head of the lake."

"Okay."

"Now, look straight from there toward the cluster of rocks that stands out by itself."

"Okay, I see it."

"That's it; there was a way into the center of those rocks, but it's closed off now."

"As good a place to rest as any I can see."

"It is and can be seen and remembered easily."

"You thought a lot of that dog, didn't you?"

"More than I realized. He saved my life more than once. On the other hand, he scared the life out of me more than once also. The cat-footed son of a gun was always slipping up on me, and out of nowhere, there he would be."

"I wish I'd have seen him."

"Look at the pup. He looks a lot like him, only I don't think the pup is quite as big. The pup shows a few of his mom's traits, too."

"He is a beautiful dog."

"That he is."

"Do you suppose he'd have hurt me the day I was reaching for your pistol?"

"I don't know. I was bluffing, but you left it alone, and I'm really glad you did."

"I believed you."

"I will never do that to you again. If I say something to you, know for sure it'll be gospel."

"I believe that, too."

"Look over there."

"At what?"

"That ledge straight over the lake were I'm pointing."

"What about it?"

"Do you see the ledge?"

"Yes."

"Can you see the cabin?"

"No."

"That's where it sits. Just so you know. There is a trail on both ends of the lake, so you can easily find your way."

"Yes, I see the trails."

"Good, let's go down. Take Anna's hand and stay close to me, and please, step carefully. It's easy enough just watch your step. It switches back and forth several times."

At the bottom, he pointed at the cave.

"Do you remember this?"

"Yes, the cave is right over there."

"Always keep a lighter or dry matches with you. There's a lantern on the rock shelf as you start in. Also, I keep a stack of firewood and some canned food in there. Always keep the tarp hooked, and there shouldn't be any problems with animals. The step going in should be high enough to keep the wild pigs out, but if the tarp is torn down, I wouldn't go in. Kind of a no-brainer."

"I understand that, use common sense always."

"Do you want to fix something, to eat or go on back to the cabin?"

"Shane's asleep, so he doesn't care. How about you Anna?"

"I'm tired. I want to go home. Will you carry me for a while?"

"I guess I can do that."

"Good. Shane has had you long enough. Mom can carry him for a while."

"It's nice to be wanted," Tonya said, and smiled.

Steve strapped Shane on her back and then hoisted Anna up onto his shoulders.

"Okay, let's go."

They went around behind the lake, so they would know the best way to go undetected, if need be. It was pretty easy walking anyway.

When they got back to the cabin, they put the children down and woke them up. They wanted them to sleep all night and not be rested up and ready to play. Steve cleaned his guns while Tanya fixed supper. Afterward, they talked into the evening while the children played under the ledge. The pup lay close and watched the children. Tonya brought out coffee and sat beside Steve on the ledge while he smoked his pipe.

"It's a perfect way to spend the evening."

"Yes, you can sit out here and relax. All your troubles just kind of disappear. Or you can think things through that you might want to do tomorrow or next week, for that matter."

"Yes, I've done that many a time myself. Do you think he'll come?"

"Don't know; do you?"

"Yes."

"How much help will he bring?"

"At least three or four, maybe more. However, many he can get in that big helicopter of his."

"How many does it hold?"

"At least six, I think, I'm not sure. It has a big cargo space on it. Maybe for five; I've really no idea for sure."

"Well, I guess we'll know soon enough. I figure it will be coming before long. Keep your eyes and ears open and remember, if something doesn't feel or look right, it probably isn't. Don't ever take anything for granted and keep your eyes on the pup. He'll let you know if something is going on as quickly as anything. Quicker than you'll ever pick up on your own."

"Anything else?"

"Yes, at the south end over there, there's a cave. My SUV is there. You'll have to hook up the battery, but if you need to, you can drive out of here. You know the way out from behind the cabin and where we might meet if we have to split up. We better keep some food packed and ready to go, just in case. I'll restock the cave with wood and canned food. Watch how much light your fire puts out at night, and God be with you, if I'm not. And if I am, with both of us."

"What about you. Where will you be?"

"I'll be okay, and unless something bad happens, I promise I'll find you. It'll be harder for you because you'll probably have both children if we're separated. The dog will probably stay with the children, but I want you to keep the nine-millimeter and extra shells with you. If he was going to kill you before, he will not hesitate to do it now."

With that, they put the children to bed and went to bed themselves. He didn't think it would be long now. The weather was nice, and things would be happening soon, or not at all. His gut feeling told him it would be soon.

Chapter 37

For the next two weeks, Steve worked from daylight till dark, trying to prepare. He put firewood and canned food in the cave, and in several other locations where Tonya and the children could hole up and be safe. At least safe from most city boys who were inexperienced in living in the wilderness.

Every night, when he returned to the cabin, he went into great detail regarding what he had done and different places they might meet, if necessary.

"Keep the nine-millimeter with you at all times. It'll be easier for you to carry and shoot over the .44 Magnum. Now all you have to worry about is the children. If someone comes, just run. Keep the pistol, children, and knife, and worry about nothing else, other than a lighter."

"Okay, I'll keep them on me at all times."

"Good. Hook the knife on your left side, and then run your belt through your pants loops and the pistol on your right and keep them there. I'll fix something for the extra clip, so you can hang that on your belt, also."

"What are you doing now?"

"I'm counting this. How much do you suppose is there?"

"I don't have any idea."

"Do you suppose that he would take the money back and just leave?"

"That would be nice, but I doubt it. He'd have a point to prove, plus the fact that he figures I know too much."

"How much do you know?"

"Not that much, really, just who everyone is and where they are, or where he lives anyway. Some of the people and places they meet. That sort of thing."

"Nothing else?"

"I had overheard some talk of people being taken care of over some bad drugs and such. People they couldn't trust anymore. Just little pieces that started adding up as the years went by. He must have realized that I had overheard a few things, and I guess he must've figured that I was becoming a problem, also."

"I'm sure you would have been better off ignorant to the facts."

"Yes, I'm sure. Anyway, that's when I started paying more attention to things. I noticed some of his help were acting sort of funny towards me. So, I started trying to find out what was going on. I heard him telling one of the men that they had to find a way to make someone disappear."

"And?"

"I wasn't sure who they were talking about until one of the older men there that I had grown close to passed me in a hallway one evening. He had always been nice to me and seemed very fond of the children. Anyway, he had gotten where he stayed completely away from us for a while. Then, on passing one evening, he never even looked in my direction, but I barely heard him mumble under his breath, 'Run; it's your only chance.' He never even looked back. He just kept walking."

"Then what happened?"

"The next morning, before my husband came home from wherever it was he had been, I took some clothes out to the building where he always kept his plane. He had flown in and fueled the plane up before moving it around and parking it in the hangar before going in the house. When they went in, I placed the children and my bags in the plane."

"When I hit the runway, they were running out after me, but they were too late. I had no idea the money was in the plane, or I'd have thrown it out. At least that way he wouldn't have had any idea where I was. I'm really sorry I brought this all on you. If I could fix it, I would. I hope you know that."

"I wouldn't have it any other way. I'm happier than I've ever been in my life. I don't see how a man could ask for any more than I have; that is, if you're staying after this is all over."

"You just try to run me off. I'm going nowhere."

"Okay, that's settled. Now, my count is exactly $1 million. I think you're right, though, he can't let you live. Nor would he let me if you weren't here anymore."

Chapter 38

The next morning, Steve woke feeling very uncomfortable about something. He laid there, wide awake, just listening to her quietly breathing beside him.

What was it? His sixth sense was screaming at him, and he had that sick feeling in his stomach. She awoke and asked him what was wrong.

"Listen."

"I don't hear anything."

"I don't either, but something is wrong."

He slipped out of bed and eased the door open a crack. Looking out, he could see the sun was just breaking over the eastern wall.

"Anything there?"

"Listen," he said, then he noticed the wolf was back, and she was staring straight at the game trail where the plane had crashed. She was staring hard with her ears back, and the hair on her back was straight up.

"What's going on?"

"Look, standing there, the wolf is back."

"Oh, my, look how she's standing."

"She's trying to tell me something. Someone is in or coming into the valley. Get dressed, and you better get the children up and dressed, also. I can't see good enough yet, but if it were an animal,

I'm sure the wolf wouldn't be here. It's human; listen to the low growl in her throat."

"Where's the pup?"

"Not far, I'm betting on that. He's probably taken a stand at the bottom of the steps where I can't see him. He wouldn't get far from you and the children."

Grabbing his field glasses, he stepped out on the ledge, and when he did, the wolf ran down off the ledge and disappeared. He knew she wouldn't go far, and if he needed her for some reason, he felt she would be there. In fact, he didn't know why, but for some reason, he knew she would be. He glassed the valley over and saw nothing. Then he checked the game trail coming off the eastern wall, and there they were: six men making their way down the trail.

Tonya came out, and he handed her the field glasses.

"No, I was hoping beyond all hope this would never happen. Are you sure it's them?"

"Not sure, but we're not taking any chances. Give me your pistol."

She handed it to him and asked, "Why?"

"Just making sure it's ready. I know that you do things right, but now I feel better."

"It's ready."

"Yes, I know. Don't forget the safety; just keep your thumb on it, and you'll be all right."

"I won't."

He slid the gun in the holster and snapped the strap over the grip, so it couldn't fall out.

"Go inside and take the pup with you; there he comes now."

She turned and started for the door, then stopped. Turning back around, she ran to him and threw her arms around him, holding him tight for just a second. Then she ran back through the door. The pup was through so fast he almost knocked her down trying to get through first, as if he understood the urgency.

"Are you coming?"

"Go, I'll catch up. You've got an hour if they come straight to the cabin. I'll watch for a little bit. On second thought, I'll help you and the kids get to the top. I have plenty of time to get back down here. Maybe we'll be able to tell from up there whether it's them or not."

They hustled the children through the cave, out the top, and over the trail. He took the money with him, not wanting them to know that he had found it. He threw it back in the cave, where the cougar had stayed, and covered it with rocks.

"Where are we going Mommy?"

"Camping again."

"That will be fun."

He thought to himself how much easier it would be if they didn't have to worry about the children. Well, he'd do his best he thought as they reached the top.

They stopped and eased their heads over the edge. Handing her the glasses, he told her to take her time and study them closely. They needed to know, for sure.

She focused the glasses carefully and studied the men. After a minute, she pulled her head back and started to cry.

"What?"

"It's them."

"You're sure?"

"Yes."

"Okay, give me the glasses; they must have studied the valley some before coming. Maps of the area, I suppose. We'd have known if anyone were around. The wolf would have let us know."

"Have you heard or noticed any planes or anything flying around?"

"No."

"I haven't either."

"Wait a second; one afternoon last week, I thought I heard a plane circle on the south end and above, but I couldn't see anything. I thought no more about it. It was cloudy that day, and I just didn't think. I'm so sorry."

"It's okay; they've probably taken aerial pictures and studied them thoroughly. They probably have seen you in them, so they know you're here."

"God help us," she said, and started to cry again.

"Don't. You have to keep calm."

"You go on and find one of the caves. I've stored food and firewood in them, and you have at least an hour head start; a lot more if I have anything to say about it. Remember, on that pistol, it's a semi-automatic. After you shoot it, get your finger off the trigger, unless you intend to keep shooting. Remember to put the safety off to shoot, and back on when finished. I don't want you to shoot yourself or one of the children."

"Go now. I'll catch up by evening. If I don't, good luck and don't give up. I've explained to you how to walk out of here, and that's probably your best bet. Just keep moving."

She looked at him for a second before saying, "Please, be careful, they won't hesitate to kill you."

"I'll be careful, I promise."

With that, she turned and told the children to come with her. She stopped for a second and stared into his eyes, not saying anything.

He looked at her, and their eyes said everything that needed said. She turned and went.

Chapter 39

He stood there for a minute, watching her go before noticing the pup just standing there. He threw his hand toward the woman while looking at the pup and said, "Go." The pup seemed glad to go with them. He turned and ran hard to catch up. It also seemed to want to be with him but was having a little problem with loyalty.

He just mumbled to himself as he turned to go back. "I want you with them," he said, as he started running back down the trail to the cabin.

Stopping at the cougar's den, he thought about it for a second, grabbed the money, and took it with him.

Reaching the slab over the cabin, he heard one of the men beating on the cabin door and hollering for them to come out. Stepping toward the edge, he threw the money over and onto the lower slab, just out from the door.

He heard them talking among themselves before one man walked out and looked into the bag. After he looked, he commented that it looked to all be there. Then he looked up and saw Steve standing there, looking back down at him. He was staring directly into the barrel of the pistol in Steve's hand. He didn't move; he just stared up and asked where the woman was.

"Not here; now take your money and leave."

"Can't do that."

"It would be a good idea."

"Why, are you feeling like dying today?"

"As good a day as any I reckon."

The man looked back at his buddies, which were still under the slab where they couldn't be seen and tried to signal to them exactly where he stood.

Two men jumped out, one on both sides of the first with their guns out, and as they did, the man at the money bag rolled and raised his gun to fire.

At that moment, Steve dropped the hammer on the .44 and felt the weapon jump hard in his hand. He saw a man take the slug directly in the chest and flopped backwards before rolling off the ledge. At the same time, he was backing away where he couldn't be seen.

He couldn't believe the rest were out on the ledge, shooting at a target that wasn't there. He had backed up far enough that there was no way they could see him, let alone hit him. They emptied their guns before he jumped to his left and then ran out on the edge again. The first man he saw was standing ready but looking where he had been, not where he was. He still had a couple of rounds left; obviously smart enough not to unload his gun completely at nothing.

When he saw Steve, he swung and fired, just clipping his shirtsleeve on his right arm.

He felt the sting of the bullet and paid the man for his effort. He didn't hurry his shot, he just leveled the gun and squeezed the trigger. The man took the slug dead in the chest and was slammed back against the rock behind him.

Jumping back again, he felt his left shirtsleeve jerk, and looking up, he saw a man had slipped down from the cabin ledge and ran out into the valley, far enough to be able to see and shoot. His mistake; he was just too far for an accurate shot with a pistol. He lobbed several more shots at him, but only one came close. It was only his shirtsleeve again, but Steve felt lucky; it only takes one.

He pulled his rifle from the shoulder, and when the man looked up from changing clips, he saw the white flash from it. It was the last thing he would ever see.

By this time, the other three had jumped out from under the ledge. He had to move; enough bullets were flying his way that he knew his luck was about to run out. Only problem was, he couldn't go back up the way he had come down. There wasn't enough cover.

He turned and ran out along the ledge, toward the north end. At least he could stay far enough from the edge that they couldn't see him going in that direction. Besides, from there, the rocks and trees pretty much had the ledge hidden.

He ran to the cave at the top of the waterfall before stopping to look back. He didn't think they had figured out where he had gone yet, and he wanted to get off the ledge before they did.

Looking around, he knew there was no way up to the top, so he walked around the pool to the opposite side. Studying his situation, he knew but one way off the ledge.

He slung the rifle over his shoulder and made sure the pistol was strapped in the holster. With that, he ran as hard as he could and jumped as far out as possible, catching a pine limb. It bent at least four feet before breaking, then he was able to grab hold of another limb. This one held, and he was able to get his feet on the limb below it. He pulled himself in against the tree trunk and climbed down to the ground. Then he ran on around the front of the lake, where he could see the front of the cabin and three men walking around trying to decide obviously what their next move would be.

Steve had pulled the rope through the whole in the cabin door, so it would take a little while for them to get in. If they got through, they'd figure out which way Tonya and the children had gone, so he made a quick decision. At the edge of the lake, he laid the rifle over a rock and cited through the scope. They were close to five hundred yards away now and really had no idea if he was still up above the cabin or not.

He watched for a minute before seeing one of the men come running out of his lower shed with his kerosene can.

He flipped off the safety and held about three to four feet over the man's head. Damn if they were going to burn his cabin, he thought to himself. He squeezed the trigger and looked up at the man. The man made a half-spin in the air and then hit the ground hard.

Looking back in the scope, he could tell the man wasn't moving. *That's four*, he thought, *only two left*. He shot once more and saw the kerosene can jump. He told himself that that should take care of the idea of burning the door.

He looked hard for the others, but they had disappeared completely. They must have found a crack to slither into he told himself.

He waited just a little while before he thought he'd better get up and move on. He stayed hidden using all the cover he could to reach the east wall before disappearing into the side fields, hoping they'd think he had them covered.

He went straight down into the side canyon where the horses were and following the stream that flowed out of the lake. He stopped at the opening of the field and studied his back trail for a good half hour before moving on toward the end, where the trail split to go up to the top, and around where the water went down over the edge and disappeared into the rocks.

When he got to the top, he kept traveling on around the upper lake, staying well past where the plane was hidden.

He wanted desperately to find Tonya, but he didn't want to take a direct path to where she might be. Plus, the fact that there might be more of them out there, so he had to be careful not to blunder into them.

Above the lake and the tree line, he came across a rocky area where there weren't any trees, and he wouldn't have any trouble not leaving any tracks.

Here he stopped and ripped the bottom of his t-shirt off, making a bandage. One of the bullets had touched his arm just enough to make it bleed. He didn't want any blood dripping on the rocks, leaving any kind of a trail.

As he crossed over the rocks, he studied everything. He could see all around himself, and he stopped every now and again just to make sure he wasn't missing anything. On one of the stops, he saw movement below him. He crouched down quickly and studied the spot and was relieved to see the wolf below him. She was looking back at him as he stared down at her.

Okay, he thought, *this would help*. He would know if anyone was close as long as she was staying with him.

He started to move when he heard the sharp crack of a nine-millimeter pistol off in the direction of Tonya—or at least were he thought she might be by now. He listened closely and heard it again, and then two more times.

Chapter 40

Tonya had taken the children and traveled the same trail they had taken two weeks earlier. She heard the shooting and was beside herself with worry.

She wanted to go back to Steve and help, but she had the children to worry about. She wanted to sit down and cry for the trouble she had caused him, but she knew there was no time for that now.

Thinking as she walked, she listened to the reports of the guns. The smaller reports first and then the report of .44. There was no mistaking that. The reports from the smaller caliber pistols and then the .44 again. Then came a shot from the seven-millimeter rifle, which she had heard on more than one occasion.

This made her smile slightly. She kept walking for an hour, still worrying, and then she jerked when she heard the rifle report again, then once more. She felt a lot better, then, knowing he was still okay, because in her mind there was only one person shooting that rifle.

When she got to the game trail where they had eaten on their picnic, she stopped to think. Where was she going to try to get today, and where might Steve try to meet up with her? If the children could make the walk before dark, she decided she was going to try and make the cave where they had camped that night.

She was thinking about all this when they came. Two men jumped from the rocks and grabbed her.

"Got you now," the big man was saying.

"Now what?"

"Before I kill her, I'm going to have my fun. Take the children down the trail to the camp; I'll be along."

He had a grip on her so tight she couldn't move, so she relaxed enough just hoping that he would, too. He hadn't taken her gun or knife yet, so she told herself that she still had a chance.

The younger man grabbed the children but was a little too rough about it. That was his mistake.

When he grabbed the boy, he hurt his arm enough that he cried out. The pup wasn't there right then; he had run back the trail when the rifle fired the last time, but when the boy cried out, he was back in an instant.

The pup grabbed for the man's throat. He got his arm up just in time. It was the most horrifying sounding thing Tonya had ever heard. There was no doubt that the pup was going to kill the man. He already had pieces of meat hanging from the man's arm and had knocked him down, rolling him over and over down the trail.

The big man tossed Tonya to the side and rushed over to kick the pup off, reaching to pull his pistol out at the same time. Tonya grabbed her own pistol, aimed, and pulled the trigger—nothing. What was the matter?

The safety! Taking her thumb and flipping the safety off, she pointed and tried again. This time the gun cracked. The bullet struck the man in the right shoulder. He swung around, trying to make his arm work properly. With an effort, he pulled his pistol up to shoot.

She stood there, holding her ground, and with her legs about a foot apart, pointed her pistol directly at his chest. The way she was standing, the man knew she wasn't backing down. He tried to point the pistol at her for a shot, but she fired again. This time putting a slug directly into his chest, right above his heart.

He stared at her for a second and tried again.

She pulled the trigger again, and this time she hit directly into the heart.

His arms dropped, and he just stood there, staring at her. It was more of a death stare, but she didn't know that. He stood too long, and she shot him one more time as his knees buckled. He laid there, face down in the dirt.

She looked up and saw the pup standing between the children and the other man.

The second man was dead but didn't know it yet. She looked at him and told him to point toward their camp, and she would help him. He pointed, and she stood up, saying she was sorry. "You have no throat left; you'll be dead before I can do anything."

He stared at her for just a second and died.

She walked away from the children, bent over grabbing her knees, and threw up. She was shaking so badly she had a hard time putting the safety back on safe position before replacing the pistol back into the holster.

When her head cleared, and her stomach felt better, she walked over to the children and helped them. She stroked the pup's head for a second and said, "Let's go; someone else might be here before long. We have to move."

Surprised that the pup let her pet him, she headed around the ledge. The children followed without question, and the pup stayed very close behind.

Chapter 41

Tonya eased around the ledge, watching ahead and behind. She watched the pup as closely as anything, knowing it would tell her faster than she would know herself if anybody or anything was close by.

After another hour, she came to where the first shelter Steve had left supplies for her should be. She knew it was close, by what he had carefully explained to her. About one hundred yards after the first trail, there stood a very large pine tree with limbs extending well over the ledge.

She saw the tree well before she came to the small opening of the cave. It was well-hidden behind the tree, and after pushing a couple of limbs aside, there it was: a three-by-four-foot opening going back into a small room. It was perfect.

He had made them some small beds with pine needles and a fire pit and enough wood for a week, if used carefully.

There was a lantern on a small ledge and a water bag hanging on a piece of wood, standing up in the corner.

She built a small fire, and in no time, the room was dry and warm. The wood was very dry and made little to no smoke.

She made soup for the children and a pot of coffee. They ate their soup, laid down on the bed, and were soon asleep. They hadn't complained once about being hungry or being tired. She was very proud of them and of Steve for everything he had taught them in the short time they had been together. Also, she understood now why he expected what he did of them: listen and obey without question. You could tell he loved them dearly and would not be able to live with himself if anything ever happened to them. Especially if it was from his negligence or lack of teaching.

She had thought him too strict at first and that the children would hate him, but soon she had seen that just the opposite was true. He took the time to explain to the children everything he told them and why he had told them or what would've happened if they hadn't listened. The rest of the time he played games with them and just paid attention to them and their needs. In return, when he asked them, they would do without question.

She was deep in her thoughts when she gradually leaned back on the pine needles herself. The last thing she remembered was the pup laying down in the opening of the little room and going to sleep. She knew that they were safe for now and soon fell asleep herself. When she awoke, it was pitch black and she sensed movement in the room. Easing her hand down to the pistol, she quietly removed it from its holster.

After a few seconds, she realized it was just the pup. He must've left and came back in, lying down again.

She lit the lantern and added a couple of pieces of wood to the coals. In just a couple of minutes, the wood was burning and throwing off heat again.

She checked the children and found that they were still asleep. She covered them and went back to sleep herself, hoping Steve was okay. He should be showing up before long was her thought.

Chapter 42

Steve headed around the far north end of the valley. He was about a mile above the lake, making his way as quickly and quietly as possible, when he crossed a trail made by four wheelers and men on foot heading toward the valley.

This had to be where the men had come from that morning. As badly as he wanted to check on Tonya and the children, he decided to backtrack this trail and see just what else he was up against. Besides, if she hadn't made it, there wasn't anything he could do now, and if she was still alive, they would bring her back this way.

There would be hell to pay if any of the three was hurt. That was a promise he made to himself under his breath as he headed north on their back trail.

Upon reaching the camp about half an hour later, he carefully skirted it and saw only one old man by the fire, cooking beans and potatoes, He obviously had enough for several men.

He started to slip away when the old man asked a question: "Have you seen everything you wanted to?"

"Pretty much, why?"

"Just thought I'd ask."

"How did you know I was here?"

"Just felt your presence."

"You're good."

"It's kept me alive for a lot of years."

"Not today."

"I realize that you already have a gun on me, right?"

"That's right, and there's a wolf, not fifteen feet from you, ready to take your throat out if you do anything stupid."

"Not going to happen."

"Smart."

"How are Tonya and the children?"

"Very well the last I seen; they should be well-hidden. I'm heading that way now. If anything has happened to any of them, I'll be back, and there will be nothing left of any of you when I'm finished."

"I believe you and hope that you can hold true to your promise. Now pay attention to me. I'll be helping you if you let me. She's like a daughter to me."

"You the man that warned her?"

"Yes."

"Thanks."

"Now what?"

"Nothing. I'm letting you live for now. I have to go check on her. You're minus four men from my doings, so far. There's two I haven't killed yet, but that's going to change. I'll be going after them first thing tomorrow."

"There's two more."

"I heard Tonya's nine-millimeter earlier. I'm hoping that's good news."

"You can believe me. I do, too."

"Is your boss here?"

"Not yet; supposed to fly in tomorrow."

"Good, we'll end this tomorrow."

"Exactly where are you located? You'll need help."

"Haven't yet."

"You will, the man has gone crazy. He'd just as soon kill a person as look at them."

"Obviously, he doesn't know you helped her."

"Obviously."

"You head south in the morning, and you'll come to the top of a high wall. It drops down about seventy feet at that point. Travel east from there and stay along the edge. About a mile from there it, splits off again. There's a small trail through the brush, heading south. And you'll find a game trail that angles back and forth down into the valley. Take a straight line from there across to the lake. On the west wall is where I left the other two. They might be back here tonight. That's all I'm telling you for now."

The old man looked around and told him to tell Tonya he'd be ready to help tomorrow but got no response. He caught movement to his right and looking, he saw a wolf as it slipped out of sight.

I'll be damned, he told himself, *he wasn't lying*.

Chapter 43

Tonya woke again and checked the opening first thing. The pup was standing there, dead still. She thought a second while drawing the pistol and watching the pup.

When the pup laid back down, she put the pistol back into its holster and placed the coffee over some coals. Then she added some smaller pieces of wood to the fire and started heating up supper.

Without even looking she said, "Your supper is almost ready."

"How did you know it was me?"

"The pup told me."

"You've learned well."

"What's going on out there?"

"I left two standing. I'll finish it tomorrow. How about yourself? I heard you shoot."

"I had to kill one of them; I had no choice."

"I believe you. Are you alright?" He asked this as he walked over and put his arms around her from behind. She broke down, saying she was all right until now.

"Until now?"

"When you came in, I couldn't look at you, and now, since you put your arms around me, I've fallen completely apart inside. Thank you for holding me and waiting for me to be able to talk. You always seem to understand."

"It was terrible. I never dreamed the pup would do anything like that so quickly. He grabbed Shane by the arm and must've hurt him a little, and when he cried out, the pup came out of nowhere and took his throat out."

"I told him I'd help him if he pointed toward his camp. He pointed north, and then I had to tell him I was sorry but I couldn't help him. There was nothing I could do for him. I'll never forget the way he looked at me. Not if I live to be a hundred years old."

"North is right. I found their camp. There was an old man there cooking."

"Dave?"

"Didn't ask his name, but he did tell me he was the one that warned you."

"That's Dave."

"He said the boss would be here tomorrow. I told him I'd finish it then, and he said that he would help us."

"He will, I believe that."

"Okay, but if he even looks like he might not, I won't hesitate."

"He was always like a father to me."

"He said he feels the same way about you."

"He had told me he wanted to get away from all of it himself, but he had nowhere to go. He didn't know how to do it and stay alive. He must have decided that some things were more important than living life the way he was."

"Maybe...we'll know tomorrow."

After they ate and cleaned up, they laid down and tried to rest. She moved herself back into him, molding her body against his. When he put his arms around her and pulled her tight against himself, she broke down and sobbed again.

"I killed a man today and saw a man die after his throat had been torn out."

"You had to shoot him and the other one shouldn't have grabbed the children as roughly as he did. I don't think I'd want to grab them like that myself. I doubt that the pup would even tolerate me doing it."

"It was ghastly. I don't know how else to describe it. I'll never forget the look on his face…never."

Chapter 44

The next morning, Steve woke early and made another fire. The little room warmed quickly as he fixed breakfast.

Tonya had awoken crying several times through the night, so he let her sleep as he made coffee. The smell of it woke her up, and she tried to smile when he handed her a cup.

The children had woken and were playing quietly. The pup was lying next to them, and he noticed that the wolf was lying right outside the entrance. For some reason, she seemed to understand and was staying close by.

He really didn't know what she understood or didn't, but he was glad she was there. She seemed to always be close by when things weren't exactly right. Then you wouldn't see anything of her for weeks on end.

After they had eaten, he took a rag and wiped off both rifle and pistol before starting out.

"What are you going to do?"

"Finish it."

"How?"

"Don't know yet. I guess I'll play it by ear."

"Wait for us."

"No! You have to stay here with the children. If I'm not back by evening to get you, go to the next cave I've set up for you, grab up everything you can carry, and head out. East is the best way to go. You'll eventually come to a highway and then go south. You'll come to a little town, and there you'll have to find a sheriff. Tell him everything other than about the man you shot. It's your only chance."

"What about you?"

"There's only one thing that will keep me from getting back. So, try to get out of here. You'll have a tough time of it with the little ones, but they're game and won't give up. They'll keep going as long as you let them set their own pace."

"I left enough money in the cave at the north end and a backpack for you. Their camp is directly north of the cave, maybe a mile, so you'll have to be careful through there. There's no other way out, and you'll have several miles of walking before you get to any kind of a road. If you can, get back to the SUV and drive out. Good luck, and please, be careful."

With that he started out. She caught him before he got out of the opening. She held him tight for a minute and then looked him in the eyes before saying, "Nothing's changed?"

"No, nothing has changed." He walked back over to the children and hugged them both.

"Mourning Dove, you and Little Bear mind your mother. You hear me?"

"Yes, father, we will."

This remark hit him hard. He swallowed the lump back down and told Little Bear, "You take care of your sister."

"He smiled big and said, "Okay, Dad."

With that he got up and left without another word. He felt his eyes water and didn't want Tonya to see.

Chapter 45

Walking along the ledge, he came to the split in the trail, and there he found the two dead men Tonya had told him about. It wasn't a pretty sight what the pup had done to the young man's arm and throat. Big mistake.

Looking around he decided to take the trail that came out above the cabin. He'd be able to see more from above.

Before he got there, he heard a helicopter coming in from the south. He ducked in behind some rocks and laid low until he knew for sure what was happening.

They landed in the valley in front of the cabin, so he went on. When he arrived above the cabin, he eased his head over the ledge and watched with his field glasses.

Four men had gotten out of the helicopter, and two more were walking to it. No doubt, the two he hadn't killed the day before. They must have camped under the ledge or maybe stayed in the cabin, which he doubted. The door was too thick to break through, and he was sure they had given up on burning it.

He watched for a minute and noticed one man handing another some dynamite with a timer. The man turned and headed for the cabin, so he put a hole in the center of his forehead. The other four emptied their weapons at the location they thought he might be in.

The second they stopped to reload, he rolled back into sight and placed a lead pill into the chest of the other man. If he could help it, they weren't going to blow the place up.

He rolled back just in time to keep from getting shot as the bullets were hitting all over the location from which he had just been.

Now what? he thought. He couldn't get down to the cabin or the valley. He needed to get down there. They'd be ready for him to look over the ledge now. His luck couldn't hold out from this location, and he couldn't get a shot from anywhere else.

Then he remembered that the pup had found a way up from the south end of the cabin. Backing away from the ledge, he ran that direction and disappeared into the rocks where the trail went down to the cabin.

There was a trail there that slipped around through the rocks for about fifty yards and then split off toward the mountains to the west.

He went west for maybe ten yards and found where another trail went back toward the valley and into some brush.

Getting down on his hands and knees, he crawled through the brush and eventually came back to the cliff that dropped off into the valley.

He heard the helicopter start up and saw it lift up.

He backed up into the brush and laid flat, hoping he wouldn't be seen. It flew over him twice, very low, but obviously he was well hidden.

After about a quarter of an hour, it landed again, so he slipped back out onto the ledge. He stooped low and ran along the edge, looking hard for a way down.

The rock wall ended at what looked like a drop-off to the bottom. He stopped and studied the surroundings closely. Nothing!

Walking to the edge, he looked over and could still see nothing. He walked back the opposite way for about ten feet when he saw a trail splitting off and around, then cutting back straight away again to the south, toward the end of the valley.

He thought maybe he could skirt around and at least get over to where the SUV was parked and maybe get down over there.

He stepped over a large rock before going through some pine brush when he felt his foot step down about six inches before resting on another rock.

Moving the brush to the side, he saw where another step was below that one. He stepped down and under some pine limbs, and from there, he could see the trail.

It widened out and cut back into the wall, where he thought it had just cut back and then went on around. He stepped on around where the trail zigzagged back and forth to the bottom. He was actually able to step from wall-to-wall on the way down with only a foot of space between the ledges.

He knew the pup hadn't come this way, but it was easily maneuvered and very well-hidden.

At the last, it went between a couple of boulders and under a ledge that was hidden by more pine trees.

Easing out to the edge of the pines, he could see the men arguing about something. Finally, one of the men picked up the dynamite and shoved it into the other's stomach and placed the pistol to his head at about the same time.

The man just looked at him for a second, then turned around and headed for the trail to the cabin.

Steve ran up a small path, which went up to the south end of the cabin and arrived just ahead of the man.

"I wouldn't."

The man froze. "I'm not," he said, and placed the dynamite on the slab.

"Step over to the side and sit down. Stay out of it."

"No problem."

He turned and started to walk over to where he was told. When he located Steve, he tried to pull his pistol and shoot.

Steve shot at the same time, and his bullet hit the man in the chest. The man was dead before he hit the ground, but his bullet had also hit.

It hit him in the left shoulder and spun him around. It went clear through without hitting the bone, but he couldn't lift the rifle back up. This gave the other two time to get to him before he could pull his pistol.

Chapter 46

Steve looked up into the wildest, coldest-looking pair of eyes he had ever seen. The man put a pistol to his head and pulled the hammer back.

"Where is she?"

"Gone."

"Like hell she is. Now, where is she?"

"I took her out of here a week ago. Your money's up there on the ledge. Get it and go."

"I will, but first I want the woman."

"I told you, she took enough money to get away and left. She has a week's head start on you. I don't know where she's heading, and I didn't ask, so I can't tell you anymore. So, take your money and go."

"I know she's still here. Last chance—where is she?"

"Right here."

He spun around and there she was, standing beside the helicopter. He grabbed Steve's pistol and walked down off the ledge and over to her. Dave was behind her with a gun in her back.

The other man picked up Steve's rifle and walked over dragging him with him. "Where are the kids?" he hollered.

"Hidden."

"Hidden where?"

"Let him go, and I'll tell you. You can get them and leave."

He slapped her and knocked her down, screaming, "Where?"

"Go to hell."

He bent over, grabbed her by the shirt collar, and jerked her up.

He started to bring the gun barrel down across her face when he felt the barrel of Dave's gun press against his own head.

He froze. The other man started to aim his own pistol when Steve slammed his good shoulder into him with everything he had left. His shoulder hit the man in the diaphragm, knocking the wind completely from him.

He dropped the rifle and tried to come up with his pistol while getting his breath. When he opened his eyes, he was looking into the eyes of the wolf. She'd hit him with enough force to knock him back down, flat on his back. Her teeth were bared and ready to grab him by the throat. No one had seen her come up behind them, except Steve.

Stepping on the pistol, he told him very quietly, "You might want to give me that."

The man let go of the pistol very carefully.

Steve picked up the pistol, spoke quietly to the wolf, and she moved away.

"You're a lucky man. Now, get in your helicopter."

He got up, walked over, stepped in, and hooked his seatbelt.

Dave had Tonya's husband covered and wasn't being very friendly. He grabbed him and shoved him into the helicopter, telling him to strap in.

"You're a dead man, Dave."

"Sure I am."

He looked over at the pilot and told him to get him to the hospital as soon as possible.

"What are you talking about?"

"His leg hurts really bad, and with that said, he shot him."

"Don't ever threaten me again. I killed the last man who did that, remember?"

He just screamed in pain.

"You've pushed and threatened people like this for a lot of years. How do you like it? Now get him out of here," he said and pointed his pistol at the pilot.

"Okay, I'm going."

The helicopter started as the three of them backed away. It lifted off and flew straightaway.

Tonya looked at Dave and asked, "How much time?"

"About seven minutes left."

"What are you two talking about?"

"The dynamite. Dave set the timer for twenty minutes and stuck it back in the helicopter before I hollered. There's still a lot of dynamite in that helicopter."

"He deserves it. He'd have eventually come back anyway."

They stood and watched as the helicopter disappeared. Just as it went out of sight, they saw a bright flash.

Dave smiled and said, "That's that; he won't be bothering you anymore."

Steve looked at Tonya and asked her where the children were.

"In the smoke house. We came around that way and slipped in while they were trying to make Joe there take the dynamite up and blow the door. We slipped into the lower shed and were ready to start shooting when you stopped him. Now, let's get that shoulder fixed."

•   •   •   •   •

Dave later asked if it would be okay for him to stay a couple of days before he left. He'd like to help clean things up before leaving.

"The least we can do. How'd you two get together?"

"I was where the pup and myself killed the two men when I looked up and noticed Dave standing on the other side, across from where you shot the grizzly. He walked around the north end and crawled across the rocks there, and we took the trail down and then walked in above the lake."

"I thought I told you to leave."

"I couldn't leave you."

"I'm glad you didn't, but you should have."

Dave looked up and said he had already made up his mind that he was going to help. He was tired of this guy and of the life he was living. He was no good and getting worse. Besides, Tonya and the children had grown on him, and he couldn't let him kill her, let alone raise the children to be like him.

Anna came over and sat on Steve's lap. She whispered and said that she couldn't remember this person's name, but she did remember him.

"Mourning Dove, this is your grandpa, Dave."

"Little Bear, say hi to your grandpa, Dave."

Dave had a funny look on his face but went along with it. He walked over and said "Howdy, how are you two today?" Then, before they could answer, he asked them to show him their home. "Then if you'd like, we can go fishing, if it's okay with your mom and dad."

Tonya looked up and told them that that would be fine.

Steve told him he could stay as long as he wanted or come back and visit anytime he wanted. It was up to him, and it would be his decision.

With that Dave took the children and went back outside.

One more thing Tonya told him: "Let the dogs make up to you. Don't try to make up to them. It probably wouldn't be very pretty, and whatever you do, be careful with the children. They're very protective."

"I figured that out when the one you call Pup wouldn't leave the smoke house without them."

Chapter 47

Dave spent the next two days helping clean up. The bodies were hauled several miles from the valley and buried in a deep ravine. Then, with the help of dynamite, covered then with several tons of rock and dirt.

After that they cleaned up the camp where Dave and the rest of the party had stayed. They parted ways there, and Dave carried off all evidence of them being there. He hauled everything out to the SUV they had come in with and drove away.

Steve explained to him where his SUV was parked and how to drive directly to the valley, telling him he was welcome to come and stay if he wanted.

Two weeks later, a couple of John's grandchildren showed up with John's cremated body in a well-packaged vase.

They took the body above the cabin and placed it where John had wanted to rest; a private place where he could watch over the valley. They did not understand his wishes to rest there, but Steve did. He tried to explain it to them but really thought he had failed.

They left the next day after breakfast. He told them to please feel free to come back any time they wished, and they were welcome to stay as long as they wished, but he could tell that they had no intentions of ever coming back.

A week later, Dave came back with a portable sawmill. Together they built a fine home at the south end of the valley. It stood just tall enough that a person could see clear to the north end of the valley when they were sitting on an upstairs patio.

They built an enclosed walkway that extended from the house to the cabin. This is where he ran the water lines to the house, so he could keep them from freezing.

They hauled in solar panels, and by the time they were finished, they had, for the most part, a modern log home.

Dave lived in the cabin for twenty-two years and was a perfect grandfather to all the children.

Tonya and Steve had one more child and eight grandchildren: five granddaughters and three grandsons.

Steve made a vault out of the cave at the north end of the valley. He put on glass doors and sealed the whole thing up tightly. The vault contained pictures of Mouse, the wolf, and pup on the walls. There were lamps on the nightstands, etc.

When asked why the two of them were making it so home-like, they said they knew it wouldn't matter later, but they felt good about it now.

When they both passed and were placed inside, the entrance of the cave was to be stoned shut. The bed was queen-sized, so they could both lay together.

For forty-six years, they were never apart for much more than a day at a time. The words *I love you* never had to be spoken. They just knew by the way they took care of each other.

It was in the fall after the whole family was together for a family reunion. Everybody was always there, no matter what, even Steve's children and grandchildren from Ohio, which added up to eighteen more. Twenty-nine in all and a stranger would have never known that Steve and Tonya weren't the parents of them all, for the same love was shown toward each child and grandchild.

It had been a perfect day. Good food and perfect weather. The most beautiful time of the year in the valley.

Everyone had turned in for the night.

As always Steve lay down, and Tonya molded herself back into his arms.

"Do you remember what I told you forty-six years ago?"

"Yes, I remember very well."

"Nothing has ever changed."

"Nor for I."

Sometime in the night, Steve's heart just stopped. He was ninety-seven years old.

At that instant, she awoke and knew.

She laid there for a second and silently sobbed to herself. She pulled herself back into him as tightly as possible and whispered one more time, "NOTHING HAS EVER CHANGED!"

With that she closed her eyes and never woke. She was eighty-two.

They were found the next morning in that position. A more perfect life had never been.

•   •   •   •   •

The children did as they were instructed.

They laid them on the bed in the vault in that same position and covered them. They put new batteries in the lamps and left them on. Then they sealed the glass doors before they stoned the entrance shut.

Looking around they could see the house at the opposite end of the valley.

One grandson said with tears in his eyes, "It couldn't be any better." Then, looking at the others he told them, "I'm staying."

CPSIA information can be obtained
at www.ICGtesting.com
Printed in the USA
BVHW031109311018
531655BV00036B/749/P

9 781480 959941